In memory of my late husband, IAN, who enjoyed reading *The Pretty Girls* chapter by chapter as I wrote them and who had always encouraged my writing.

Hazel Aitken lives in Fife and has been publishing short stories, articles and poems for many years. She has three adult sons and four grandchildren, and enjoys trips to co Kildare, Ireland, where some of the family live. Involved in practical charity work, she also has a passion for social history, gardening and for the cats she has rescued.

Hazel Aitken

THE PRETTY GIRLS

AUSTIN MACAULEY PUBLISHERS™

LONDON · CAMBRIDGE · NEW YORK · SHARJAH

A CIP catalogue record for this title is available from the British Library.

ISBN 9781528902441 (Paperback)
ISBN 9781528957977 (ePub e-book)

www.austinmacauley.com

First Published (2019)
Austin Macauley Publishers Ltd
25 Canada Square
Canary Wharf
London
E14 5LQ

Chapter One

Manchester 1860

"Polly killed a little baby."

Hannah, about to step from the footpath that ran beside the cobbled street and turn into the gateway leading to the house where she and her widowed mother had taken a room, stared down at her neighbour, a poorly clothed and undernourished little girl with dirt-encrusted nails and red-rimmed eyes.

"She did, miss." The child gazed up beseechingly. "I saw."

"Sal! Where is that wretched child?" A pudding faced woman, lips a tight line, appeared from behind a holly hedge that screened the house next door. "Oh, there you are, you varmint." The child's gaze slid away from Hannah but not before she had glimpsed real fear in their depths. Sal, if that was the child's name, was terrified of this angry woman.

"She wasn't doing any harm," Hannah said and held out a hand. "My mother and I are living next door. Mrs Wilson's our landlady…" She broke off and her hand fell to her side as the woman grabbed the little girl and pulled her roughly to her side. With a swift jerky movement, the child was whisked from view, disappearing behind prickly hollies that lined a path leading to a glass panelled front door from which faded brown paint peeled.

"Take that! What have I told you? You're not to set foot outside that door, you little devil." There was the sound of a sharp slap and then a high-pitched wail that was cut off quickly. Hannah had the mental vision of a hand placed over the child's mouth.

With fiery indignation and outrage, she turned towards the front door of number fourteen Blackfriar's Lane and the house where she and her ailing parent now resided. No shrubs lined the path here although next door's holly hedge was a divider. The front area was spartan and bleak but the house had known better days and possessed a glass-panelled front door and boasted a small brass hammer which Hannah lifted and let fall, summoning their impatient landlady.

"Oh, it's you. You've not been gone two minutes. Forgotten something, have you? I can't spend time running to the door whenever you lift the knocker."

"I was at least half an hour, Mrs Wilson. I don't know the area and had to find a pharmacy. My mother's cough is troublesome."

Her landlady sniffed and straightened her black serge skirt. "She's a burden is that one. Still, not long for this world if I'm any judge."

"Then I hope you are not. My mother has been through too much of late but she will pull through." *And no thanks to you,* ran her thoughts. *The place is as cold as a morgue and about as cheerful.*

"May I remind you, young lady, that the rent is due in two days' time? If you can't pay, the pair of you are out of here."

"We can pay." Hannah held her head high as she passed Mrs Wilson and made her way towards the stairs that led to a well-sized landing onto which several doors opened. However, the attic room she and her mother could barely afford was accessed by narrow, uncarpeted stairs and the sound of Hannah's boots echoed.

"Is that you, Hannah?" Her mother's thin voice called from within a room that was poorly furnished and through which spiteful draughts whistled. "I thought you'd got lost."

Daylight filtered through a small window that looked over the back of the house and peering at an angle Hannah could see a little of the next-door backyard. Not that she had any intention of doing so at the moment. Her mother was the priority as a bout of coughing drained her strength and left her gasping in the chair where she sat wrapped in a woollen blanket.

"This may help." Hannah poured cough tincture onto a spoon and handed it to Belle Morley. "The apothecary on the main street says it is their own concoction and most effective."

"You're a good girl and I'd be lost without you," Belle said, "but no twenty-year-old should be in your position."

"Nonsense." Hannah shed her knee-length cloak and hung it on a hook on the back of the door. Then she smoothed her straight dark hair. "Plenty of girls are far worse off. But you realise I shall have to find work. Our money is running out. I have paid Mrs Wilson to supply some food but it won't be enough. There's a chophouse not far away but I'm not sure we can afford meat."

"I am a terrible burden, God knows. Oh, if only your dear father had not been killed in that dreadful accident and if only he had made better provision for us. Of course, he was too generous for his own good, or ours. Attending all those patients and never accepting a penny…"

Hannah had heard it all before a hundred times. How her father, a doctor, had attended all and any in the area who required his skills whether or not the patient was in a position to pay. Twelve months earlier, a runaway horse and carriage had ended his life soon after he had attended an accouchement in a nearby village. For his sake Hannah was glad that he had not been left a helpless cripple but she mourned him deeply. A year was no time at all and she walked with grief although some doubted it because Hannah did not wear deep mourning.

From early childhood her father, so often frequenting homes where death had visited, had informed her that he loathed the black clothes donned by the bereaved and considered it an affront to the dead. "If their lives were tolerably happy, we should celebrate them and if the reverse we should rejoice that they are in a better place."

If she was entirely honest, she was not sure how deeply her mother grieved although the unrelieved black she wore, including a mourning veil when she stepped outside, might indicate a depth of suffering of which she was incapable. Belle could be very introspective and as her health was not robust, she had become more self-absorbed since her widowhood began. Much of her time had been spent in fretting about her physical condition, but to be fair she was probably consumed with anxiety about their future and the fact that she was in no position to alleviate their hardship. If they were to survive and stay out of the workhouse, it would be because Hannah took control.

"I met the little girl who lives next door," she told Belle in order to fasten the woman's thoughts on something other than her current poor health. "I think she is called Sal. That's what the woman called her."

"Tell me about her, dear. Is she pretty?"

"I'm not sure. I mean, yes, but she was upset. She was also very dirty." It occurred to her that to describe the scene might distress Belle. "I think she had escaped to play outside. Something like that, and the woman, maybe her mother, was very cross with her. I felt rather sorry for her. She seemed a lonely little thing."

"You were probably lonely too as an only child. Of course, I would have liked another one but it didn't happen. Besides, it might have killed me. I was never very strong. Oh, isn't it cold? And I swear I heard mice scrabbling in the walls. I hate this place."

"Me too, and I am perfectly sure you *did* hear mice. After all, we are in the attics but we can afford nothing else."

Sometimes Hannah felt impatient with her mother. After all, she was doing her best for them both and all too often Belle moaned and bewailed their circumstances. Of course, it was quite dreadful living in a smoke-filled city after breathing fresh country air all their lives, but things might have been worse. She had read and heard of families crowded into cellars, absorbed into a city that required labour but found itself bearing the burden of poverty and disease. She knew that cotton mill owners had invested in expensive machinery and although they paid relatively good wages, the workers were exhausted by long shifts; then there were the unemployable. Some poor souls always fell through the net.

"Yes, I would have liked another baby. Babies are so sweet, so helpless…"

But Hannah was not listening. Another voice, Sal's, was echoing in her mind. "Polly killed a little baby." Whatever had the child meant?

"You're new around here, aren't you? Settling in, then?" The apothecary's assistant was a cheerful young man not much older than Hannah. Pale blonde hair flopped over a wide forehead and he seemed to wear a permanent smile which brightened his somewhat gloomy surroundings. The shop's interior was painted brown and dominated by a long counter of the same colour. Weighing scales and a pestle and mortar took up one end and behind it, shelves were crammed with bottles and jars, pots of salve, and overall hung the aromatic scent of herbs. If Hannah found it somewhat claustrophobic, she also found it of great interest. Owing to her late father's profession, she was familiar with many of the medicinal products and aids, and during her growing years had often watched him at work in his own small dispensary.

She had learned that the young man's name was Samuel. "Sam to my friends," he'd told her. "You may call me that if you wish. But I wouldn't be so bold as to ask your Christian name Miss Morley." She had not enlightened him on such brief acquaintance

"Thank you, Sam." She held out her hand for yet another bottle of cough mixture. Not that it was doing her mother much good but that was probably less to do with the medicine than the penetrating cold that drained her parent of strength. Too much energy was being used in a futile attempt to keep warm, but its contents, one of which was laudanum, made her mother drowsy and took the edge off her discomfort.

"I should like some herbal tea too, nettle, I think. Well, we haven't really settled. Our lodgings are…well, let's say not what we were used to, but I expect you can guess how it is. Frankly, I need to find work."

"Samuel Webster, I don't pay you to talk. Take the young lady's money and get on with your job."

"That's the boss, Mr Lawson. He's in the back room stirring his poisons! Eyes in the back of his head, he has. Probably in a few other places as well, I shouldn't wonder. Thank you," he added as Hannah passed over a handful of small coins. "I'll give the matter some thought. You don't look as if you're used to being in service."

Hannah shook her head and was about to reply when the boss emerged from behind a green curtain that shielded an inner door. Sharp eyes took in her appearance and his long aquiline nose seemed to quiver. "Good day," she said quickly and stepped outside to find it was now raining so causing her to lift her skirts to avoid them being dragged along wet and dirty pavements. It seemed there was no end to misery and this was re-enforced when a passing carriage splashed filthy water and stained them. Then, on reaching their lodgings she had to bear the brunt of Mrs Wilson's sharp tongue and after toiling upstairs found her mother in a state of agitation and despair.

"It's the mice again. Well, to be honest I think it is a rat. I heard such strange noises in the wall."

"Rats and mice squeak. Is that what you heard?" Hannah did not mean to sound impatient but it occurred to her that Belle lacked what one would call backbone. Sometimes she was as helpless and complaining as a small child. Papa had doted on her, his sympathetic nature responding to her real or imagined weaknesses, but Hannah would have admired a more sturdy spirit.

You're not a very nice person, Hannah Morley, she told herself and having shed her wet outer garments, set about boiling water on a small inefficient burner Mrs Wilson had supplied with many a grumble. "That'll be two pence extra a week," she had finished, "and if your mother requires broth at midday, that'll be another three pence." *Yes, I shall have to find work*, Hannah told herself for the umpteenth time.

"Can you hear that?" Belle sat up a little and a thin hand cupped her ear. Hannah straightened to attention. There were indistinct sounds coming through the wall, echoing from the adjoining house. She supposed, but they were muffled and unclear.

"Well, whatever or whoever is making a noise, it is not a mouse or rat, that's certain," Hannah said stoutly. "It sounds like…well. I'm not sure, someone crying maybe. Perhaps one of next door's servants has received a reprimand and is distressed. Or…" she came to a halt as the thought crossed her mind that the child Sal might have been banished to the attics for some misdemeanour.

"Someone is in pain," Belle said firmly. "I should know. Quite definitely someone is calling out in pain."

"Here, drink your nettle tea. It's full of goodness, so I believe, and try not to worry about mice, rats or goings-on next door."

Belle threw her a glance which indicated she thought her daughter was being hard-hearted. *Far from it*, thought Hannah whose ears were straining for the sounds of distress that were becoming more evident. Someone was wracked with pain and she longed to break down the dividing wall and offer assistance. Was it little Sal? She thought not. A long drawn out moan seemed decisive. No child, then, but who lay the other side of the attic wall?

As she seated herself on the edge of the lumpy mattress she shared with her mother and lifted a cup of herbal tea to her own lips, one shriek of pure agony caused her to start with alarm.

"Heavens above! Someone is dying, Mama."

"One does not make that noise when in extremis," Belle remarked unfeelingly. "I should know."

"You've never been in extremis. Had you been, you'd not be here." Hannah tried to make the remark light-hearted but knew her impatience showed. "I am sorry, Mama. It is just that I am anxious about our future. I am wondering how best to combine a working life with our lives here."

"What you mean is that if you were not burdened with me, you would be free to find employment further afield or take a live-in position." Belle's lips drooped self-pityingly. Then changing the subject she remarked, "It's quiet now. Perhaps the person who made such a noise is now sleeping."

Hannah drained her cup. "Perhaps, Mama. But it seems no place for a child and the more I think of that awful woman who pulled Sal indoors, the more anxious I am about the child. I feel I should find out more about her."

"Leave well alone, my dear, is my advice. Even if the mite is beaten black and blue, there is nothing you can do about it. It's a parent's right to chastise their child and no constable would listen to you."

Hannah sighed. Her mother spoke the truth. Besides, she had enough troubles without looking for more.

****

Chapter Two

Mrs Wilson appeared less approachable than usual when next Hannah descended the stairs and entered the big gloomy kitchen. The house, built a hundred years previously, whilst not obviously neglected, showed no signs of being tended with care, and this room in common with others Hannah had glimpsed, was grimly austere. Even the coals in the stove failed to glow. They spluttered and hissed as if damp.

"Is it possible to have another blanket? My mother feels the cold most dreadfully and as you know there is no fireplace in the attic room so we cannot burn coals."

"It'll cost you. Another two pence. This isn't a charity, though it might as well be a doss house."

A movement in the scullery beyond caught Hannah's eye and for the first time she noticed a young girl, possibly no more than ten years old, standing on a box at a low stone sink. Small hands grappled with large potatoes as the child peeled the vegetables with a knife that gleamed.

"Of course I will pay you." Hannah delved into a fabric purse she had with her and Mrs Wilson held out a thin hand.

"I'll see what I have; wait here." Hannah did as she was bid and no sooner had the woman disappeared into the hall than she called to the child in the scullery.

"Hello! My name's Hannah. What is yours?" There was no verbal response but the child turned her head in Hannah's direction. Impossible to see the colour of her hair because her head was encased in a grey cap that almost fell over her eyes. Eyes that darted here and there as if enemies lurked in every corner and might assault her at any moment.

"Don't be frightened. I won't hurt you. My mother and I are living in one of the attic rooms. Maybe you will come upstairs and call upon us sometime." There was a vigorous shaking of the head and the girl nearly fell from the box.

"Here we are and it's the best I'm prepared to offer." Mrs Wilson had reappeared. Over her arm hung something that in Hannah's opinion resembled a horse blanket. *And it's the colour of dung, poor Mama.* "Were you interrupting Leary?" continued the woman. "The brat is slow enough without you holding her back."

"Leary? Is that her name?"

"What's it matter? Workhouse off-loaded her. One of the guardians knew someone who knew me and the child should thank her lucky stars I took her in. Glad to be rid of her I daresay. As if I haven't enough to do without teaching her the basics of housekeeping."

Hannah took the blanket and wrinkled her nose. It gave off a most unpleasant odour which she could not place; metallic, maybe?

"Don't turn your nose up at it." Mrs Wilson had not missed her expression of repugnance. "Next door were throwing it out and I say waste not, want not."

"In which case I doubt you'll ever want, Mrs Wilson."

"Don't get smart with me, young woman. I could have you and your mother out in the street in an instant. And you, Leary, get on with those vegetables. Then you can scrub the stairs." The child's head sank low and Hannah's heart did the same. What a fate to be under Mrs Wilson's thumb.

"Goodbye Leary, although I guess you have another name and one day you shall tell me. And thank you, Mrs Wilson." *For what? A miserable smelly old horse blanket, you horrible woman.*

Upstairs, her mother recoiled when Hannah proffered the blanket. "It smells appalling, my dear. Is that the best you could do?"

"Yes, Mama. Our glory days are over so it is indeed the best I could do. Mrs Wilson is a ..." It was on the tip of her tongue to use a forbidden word but *that* woman, as she was beginning to think of her, brought out the very worst. Remote, unfeeling, grasping and lacking any compassion, when in fact she had it in her power to bring comfort into the lives of Leary, her mother and herself.

I have to get us out of here, ran Hannah's thoughts. *I have to find work and lift us out of this pit of misery.*

"I refuse to have that thing near me," rose her mother's querulous voice. "It's got blood stains on it and now I come to think of it, there's a smell of blood too. Take it away, Hannah, I would rather freeze to death."

Hannah turned away from Belle so that the other should not see the tears of frustration and despair that filled her eyes. Since the day her father had been killed, their lives had taken a downwards spiral. There was no living relative to help them; there had been no business partner, and owing to her father's philanthropy and, if she was honest, his careless approach to his finances which had left them in debt, they had been compelled to leave the attractive rented house in the village of Longwell ten miles away and move into the city which seemed to have swallowed them up. Their previous landlady, a widow named Mrs Mariah Simpson, had been sympathetic and kindly, her concern obvious, but she required the income from the rented house left to her by a relative, and after three months had slipped past, Hannah and her mother had moved out.

"I can store some of your furniture until you find somewhere permanent," Mrs Simpson had offered. "There is attic space in my own house." So, it had been arranged and several of the better pieces now resided in Mrs Simpson's modest home where, they were assured, a welcome always awaited.

"Her attics were better than these," moaned Belle on many an occasion. "We might have thrown ourselves on her mercy. In the past year we've gone from bad to worse. You are too proud, Hannah, and that's the truth of it. Telling her we should soon settle elsewhere. What about me?"

"It will be all right, Mama, wait and see. I intend to look for employment as soon as possible. And the first thing I shall do is buy you a soft blanket. It was a pity we parted with most we possessed but we needed the money and now it is fast running out."

Tomorrow, she thought, she would begin looking for a suitable occupation, and she would begin by asking Sam at the apothecary's if he had any good ideas.

Sam was busy with the pestle and mortar, once again pounding ingredients at the counter. He greeted Hannah with a cheerful grin and pushed back his unruly fair hair.

"How's your mother? Cough any better?"

"Slightly, I think, but I am not here for medication. I need advice, Sam." Her gaze flickered towards the inner door. "I don't want to get you into trouble by taking up your time."

"I don't get away until eight, sometimes nine of an evening. Best get it over with…I mean…"

"I know what you mean. I need work, Sam, as you know. Did you have any bright ideas?"

"There's the big old workhouse out Bronton Way." He noticed her shocked expression and hastened to explain. "You'll be familiar with the big one on New Bridge Street, but this one is undergoing change, real change. There's a new master, money available for renovations, and they need staff. Teachers, nurses, those sort of people."

"Samuel Webster, are you slacking again?" His elderly thin faced boss emerged through the doorway. "You again, miss? What is it this time? Hold a candle for my assistant, is that it?"

It took Hannah a moment to grasp his meaning and then she blushed. "I was asking Sam, Mr Webster I mean, if he knew of any work? I need to earn some money."

"Well, *he* won't be earning if he keeps leaving off what he's doing to speak to you. Anyway, I doubt he knows the meaning of the word work!"

Now it was Sam's turn to blush and he opened his mouth to protest but with a smile that included both of them, Hannah left the premises and hurried back to Belle.

"Miss, help me, miss." It was Leary who opened the front door when she knocked upon it. "I've cut me thumb real bad." She had too. Blood dripped through a dirty looking cloth onto the tiled floor of the hall and Hannah put an arm around the child.

"Where's Mrs Wilson?" she asked. "Can't she help you?"

"She's gone out, miss. Said she'd be a while which usually means a couple of hours. Oh, do help me…" She ended on a wail and Hannah hustled her upstairs and into the attic room.

"Look who we have here, Mama. This is Leary who works here and she is hurt. Sit down," she ordered and the little girl sat on the low bed. "Now, what can we use as a bandage? I know, my old shift. I'll tear a piece off the hem. Take off that filthy rag, my dear."

Without shedding her cloak and bonnet, she pulled a trunk from its place in the corner and finding what she sought, ripped a good-sized piece from it. Having poured water into a tin bowl, she dipped a piece of material into it and proceeded to examine the wound.

"However did you do this, Leary? It's deep and you'll need to keep it clean and dry." With gentle wipes she washed the cut as best she could, applied a salve which had also been in the trunk, and bandaged the thumb.

"My Hannah's good at that sort of thing," Belle remarked with a touch of pride. "What did you say your name is, child?"

"Mama, I told you she is named Leary. But I think that's only part of it. Have you another name?" she asked, her hand on the girl's thin shoulder.

"Don't know, miss. That's what they called me at the work'ouse, the Bronton place."

Belle had turned to face the child, what light there was entering through the small window shone on the small, scared face.

"Did she say workhouse? The poor child. How old are you, dear?"

"They told Mrs Wilson I was nine or ten," was the whispered reply, and then as if the woman's name had brought Leary face-to-face with the reality of her situation, she slid off the bed. "I gorra go back downstairs. I got work to do or she'll be mad as a box of snakes."

"I shall accompany you. Just let me take off my cloak and we'll go down and wait for Mrs Wilson."

Leary looked uncertain, but Hannah steered her out of the door and led the way down to the gloomy kitchen. In the scullery were half-peeled vegetables and a pool of blood in the old stone sink.

"I gorra get on, I must really." Leary sounded desperate but Hannah told her to sit down in the kitchen.

"You're still bleeding. Look, it is seeping through the bandage already. You need a cup of hot sweet tea and I shall finish your chores. With any luck, Mrs Wilson will think you completed them. And if she returns, I shall take the blame. Thank heavens the kettle manages to boil on this miserable stove."

A few minutes later, Leary sat sipping tea. "I like me tea strong. Not that I get anything but the dregs usually, miss, but me spoon could stand up in this!" Hannah smiled as she scrubbed the sink clean of bloodstains. Then she finished scraping a heap of vegetables and set to cleaning the scullery floor and kitchen shelves. "Mrs Wilson will think the fairies have been in to help," she said, hoping to raise a smile. It was a futile attempt and after a minute she gave up.

"Leary, dear, do you know how you came to be in this area? I think with a name like that, you must have come from Ireland, or maybe your parents did?"

"I'm not sure, miss. I think I had people come over from somewhere because they were hungry. There was a famine, like in the Bible, someone at the work'ouse said. But it was all a muddle what they told me."

"That sounds like Ireland. There was a terrible famine. More than one but the worst was fifteen years ago or so. Starving people poured into English cities. My father thought the government could have done more to help the Irish but he was the sort who helped everybody."

"Like you, then miss. You help people. Look how you've helped me." She had drained the tea mug and looked relieved when it had been washed and replaced on a small dresser. "I think you'd better go, miss."

"If you're sure…" Too late they heard the front door slam and Mrs Wilson calling for Leary.

Taking the child by the hand, Hannah propelled her into the hall where they met Mrs Wilson's outraged gaze. "You! What are you doing, may I ask? Stop mollycoddling that girl. Carry on like that and discipline flies out of the window."

"Leary has cut her thumb very badly, Mrs Wilson. Fortunately, the kitchen work is completed and I have done my best to dress the injury, but I don't think she will be able to use her hand much. She must not get the cut wet or infection may set in."

"Miss Know-It-All!" scoffed the woman. "And how come you *do* know so much? Here, Leary, take my mantle and quick about it." She tossed the garment and the child caught it, wincing as pain shot through her thumb.

"My father was a physician," Hannah told her, her attention caught by something she had noticed. There was blood on the cuff of the grey dress Mrs Wilson was wearing. She too must have suffered a small injury.

Did she imagine a shadow cross her landlady's face, a moment of indecision as if she might have ventured another comment? If so, the moment passed.

"I am very willing to dress Leary's hand until the wound has healed," Hannah said.

"That will not be necessary. I am perfectly capable of dealing with such trivialities."

Hannah pressed Leary to her. "Be brave," she whispered as she bent over her. But Mrs Wilson was having none of it.

"You keep to your own room and leave the child to me. I'd say you've more than enough on your plate with your ailing, wailing mother. Mollycoddle *her* if you like, but don't interfere in my affairs."

****

Chapter Three

It was twice in a morning that the Bronton workhouse had been mentioned and although Hannah quailed at the very name, she found herself wondering whether a solution to her financial problems might lie within. If they *were* recruiting staff and if she was permitted to stay with her mother overnight and attend to her needs before beginning a day's work, it might prove successful. There was only one way to find out and that was to enquire. And only one way to do that. She didn't even know where the place was situated, having heard only vaguely that it was two or more miles distant, but she would make her way there and instead of pestering Sam Webster, she would ask his employer for directions.

Leaving Belle with all that she might require close to hand and having wrapped her as warmly as was possible, Hannah took her leave and walked briskly towards the main thoroughfare where potential customers stared into shop windows and a few carts were drawn up alongside the pavement. Sam's face lit up when he saw her enter the apothecary's, but his expression fell when she asked to speak to his employer.

"It's about employment. I don't want to get you into trouble but I need advice. I shall have to flatter him, won't I?" Her smile was disarming. "What is his name? If I knew it, I have forgotten."

A minute later, she was explaining her predicament to Sam's stern looking employer. "You see, Mr Lawson," she finished, "I believe the Bronton workhouse is undergoing changes and requires staff. Teachers, maybe?"

"Come into the back room, we cannot converse here." He led the way into a smaller room where shelves were piled with books and glass jars containing specimens and what appeared to be animal remains suspended in fluid. "I am keeping an eye on you, Samuel Webster," he called and left the dividing door open.

21

"Sit," he went on and pulled forward a battered wooden chair whilst he continued, "It's true there *is* a new master with big ideas." He sniffed. "A Yorkshire man, I'm told, one of these non-conformist do-gooders with a scheme to improve the lot of the poor."

"Isn't that worthy? Their lives are bleak enough, heaven knows." Leary's little face came to mind, quickly followed by that of Sal next door.

Mr Lawson sniffed, his long nose quivering, but he made no further comment on the subject. Instead, he studied Hannah and she felt like one of his specimens. "You look healthy enough. No doubt they can do with nurses in that place. Hundreds of inmates, all ages and conditions. Are you familiar with such establishments?"

Hannah shook her head and a strand of dark hair brushed her cheek having escaped her bonnet.

"No, only what I have heard. I daresay I could nurse, I know the basic rules because my father was a physician, but I may be more suited to teaching. I am quite well educated."

She did not have to explain herself to this man but she needed his cooperation. The more she could learn about the workhouse the better. "Hundreds of paupers, you say?"

"Segregated. Wards and areas for men and women, for the children too. Wards for the lunatics and violent inmates and the sick, a lying-in ward and so I could continue. Put you off, have I?

"I'm not sure, Mr Lawson. I mean someone has to care for these people and that someone might as well be me. The children will need attendants and teachers, surely?"

He stood up and she sensed dismissal so rose to her feet. "...continue past the old church. You can't miss it, being renovated, you see... I'll draw you a map; less trouble than explaining. When you get there, don't go to the vagrant's entrance. The principal entrance is on the other side of the building. There's a bell to summon the porter."

In the shop Sam was attending to a pair of middle-aged ladies and his glance was perfunctory. Mr Lawson accompanied Hannah to the door and after thanking him once more, she was in the busy street. It was not a fashionable area and some way from the city centre, but there were rows of shops and horse-drawn vehicles constantly blocking one another's route. Half an hour later and with the ancient church behind her, Hannah noticed that the houses and shops were thinning and in places fields and allotments bordered the road. Then the sprawling buildings comprising the workhouse came into view, daunting and forbidding. One could only imagine the dread and trepidation with which bereft persons on parish relief or in failing health entered the place.

As she drew close, Hannah heard the sounds of men at work and coming to the gatehouse saw in a yard beyond teams of workmen, thin tired-looking horses pulling goods wagons laden with building supplies. All around seemed noise and commotion; voices raised, shouted instructions, the clatter of materials being unloaded. This had to be the principal entrance and with her heart drumming fast, she lifted an impressive brass door knocker.

She was not sure what she expected but the porter, if such he was, opened the door swiftly. A middle-aged man with shaven face and somewhat downtrodden appearance surveyed her, and she explained her business.

"Cross the yard, miss. Go to the door you see over there. Ask for the matron, Mrs Stannard. She's a busy woman, no need to tell you that, but she's taking on staff, that I do know."

Hannah skirted around the labourers, horses and wagons, and minutes later was being admitted to the main block by a surly grey-haired woman who unlocked the door to admit her, and re-locked it behind her. She was shown into an office and told to wait, which she did for a full half an hour, during which time she came to know the contents of the shadowy room very well; the cracked paintwork and piles of books and ledgers littering a broad desk; wooden shelves in danger of collapsing. The atmosphere was depressing.

Not so the woman who eventually entered the room, a hand outstretched in welcome and Hannah's own was grasped firmly. "I am Mary-Anne Stannard, matron here, and you are…?" *She's about thirty-five, mousey colouring but she's anything but mousey,* thought Hannah.

"Hannah Morley. I am twenty years old, have the care of my widowed mother and I need to find work. Someone told me you were engaging staff."

The other woman's keen glance took in Hannah's blue woollen dress that matched the colour of her eyes, the well-worn cloak, her neat bonnet and clean appearance. "Tell me more, Miss Morley."

Hannah did, then sat back with a sigh. "So you see, I cannot leave my mother completely unattended, but if there was a position that would permit me to be with her overnight, and if I was offered such a situation, it might be possible for me."

"It might be entirely possible. Quite apart from maids, orderlies and attendants, the master and I are engaging two teachers, more nurses…but really, *their* work consists of mopping up and cleaning both bodies and floors, a tailor and his assistants, a cook who will make something more nourishing than thin vegetable broth…oh, I could go on. You are educated, you tell me. Explain."

"My mother taught me to read, write, paint, embroider and play the pianoforte. Then, along with a couple of other local children, I received lessons from the tutor at Longwell Hall in his free time. He taught us mathematics, geography and English history."

"Is there anyone in Longwell who might provide you with a reference, Miss Morley?"

"Yes, I am sure of it. The rector, an elderly gentleman now, the Reverend Horatio Lovatt-Browne, and our ex-landlady, Mrs Mariah Simpson."

"Then I suggest you write to them. I think if all is satisfactory, you may be offered a position as a teaching assistant to some of the girls. Let us take one step at a time. There are such changes going on here, it is quite breath-taking." Her pale face lit up and her eyes sparkled. "Mr Gidley is master here, a man from north Yorkshire. With funding approved, he has such plans to make sweeping changes for the better. Good gracious, I am getting carried away! But these *are* exciting times and if you join us, you will see for yourself. So…you get down to obtaining those references. What will be, will be. Any questions?"

"None that I can think of, but the place is so much cleaner and better organised than I had supposed."

Mrs Stannard laughed. "I'm afraid that is not really the case and never will be. How could it be when so many people live in close proximity and with such a variety of human ills? But we are making a start, Mr Gidley and myself. This place was an anteroom to hell, believe me, but no longer. I do believe that with the good Lord's help, we shall overcome the worst. Goodbye for now, Miss Morley."

*****

Back in the attic room, Hannah brewed tea and handed Belle a cup.

"You were gone for hours, my dear. What kept you? Mrs Wilson brought me broth an hour since."

"Looking for employment, Mama, and I may have found it." She started to tell her mother of the morning's adventures but Belle's lips tightened.

"No child of mine is going to mix with vagrants, and coarse rough people who never soap their skin. Do not speak of it, I beg you."

"Very well, Mama, we shall not speak of it."

"And do not pursue the idea," her mother continued. "I know you, Hannah. When you get an idea into your stubborn head, you are like a runaway horse."

Hannah went to the trunk and produced writing paper, ink and a quill pen. "Quite right," Belle said, "Write and tell whoever it is that you are not going to consider employment in a workhouse. I don't know what came over you."

"The threat of poverty, Mama. That's what came over me. If you wish to know, I am writing to our old rector and to Mrs Simpson for references. For whether or not I am engaged at the workhouse, I shall require them. Now, please, let me consider what to write."

Belle sighed with annoyance but kept silent. Finally, satisfied with the results of her labours, Hannah read aloud what she had written.

14 Blackfrairs Lane
Manchester.
20th November 1859

"Dear Mrs Simpson,
I trust all is well with you as it is for ourselves. Mama has been unwell but is somewhat recovered from a chesty cough and I am in excellent health.
We have lodgings at the above address but it is necessary for me to obtain references as I propose to earn my living by teaching infants. I hope you will feel able to give me a good character reference.
Mama asks that she be remembered to you and wishes you well, as do I.

Your affectionate friend,
Hannah Morley

"I have written in much the same tone to the rector but have requested that he comment on my academic abilities," she told Belle. "Now I am going to post these when I have sealed them. I am sure we have sealing wax in the trunk. Ah, here it is. Now for the striking match."

"New-fangled things," grumbled Belle half-heartedly but Hannah made no reply, her thoughts leaping ahead to the replies she anticipated in response to her letters

Belle was certainly improving, in health if not in temper. Her list of complaints was not without foundation, for the trek to the outside privy was tedious and unpleasant, the backyard awash when it rained and there followed the ascent of narrow attic stairs to their room. To add to her misery were the dishes provided by their landlady, thin, gruel and something resembling dishwater that passed for soup. Then too there was the boredom she endured.

Hannah did her best to alleviate her predicament, helping her up and downstairs, buying bread and meat and cheese and the occasional chop from a nearby establishment, but her mother's empty hours were difficult to fill.

"Mama, if we place your chair beside the window, there may be enough light by which to read or sew. Let's do it now." She hauled Belle out of the chair and then moved the furniture around. "That's better. All right, you do not wish to sew, but I will obtain books for you. I imagine there is a circulating library and I shall find it, and I think we should attend a church. It will benefit us in every way and provide another interest. Maybe the Reverend Lovatt-Browne could suggest one in the area."

"I am not sure, my dear. In Longwell we had some standing and my clothes were attended to. Here, I feel at a great disadvantage. It makes me irritable, I know, and then I feel guilty."

"Poor Mama. I feel the same, but things *will* change. Wait and see." A cry from Belle interrupted the conversation.

"Hannah, quickly dear, come to the window. There's a poor child out in next door's yard and she must be freezing. Oh, it isn't right, not at all. She's wearing hardly a stitch."

"That's Sal, the little girl I told you about. You remember, the child who was pulled indoors and slapped. I am sure of it." Hannah stared down into the one corner of the yard that was visible. A pile of rubbish filled most of it and huddled next to it was Sal, thin bare arms clutching a poor-looking shawl around her shoulders. "Mama, I do believe she has no boots. She must be so cold. Whatever monster would condemn a child to such treatment? I have a good mind to go next door and demand that the child be brought in."

"You would get short shrift, I have no doubt. Oh, it is pitiful, quite dreadful. Let us devise a plan to make her lot a little easier. Have you any ideas? You are usually full of ideas, Hannah."

"Well…suppose you cut down one of the dresses in the trunk and sewed a garment for her. It wouldn't matter if it was a trifle too big. A sash around the waist would fix that. I could hand it in and tell some story as to how we came to have it."

Belle glanced up with more enthusiasm in her eyes than Hannah had seen since her father's death. This was more like the mother she knew; compassionate if rather self-absorbed. "Look in the trunk, dear. Do look."

A few minutes later, Belle was examining a tartan dress that Hannah secretly disliked owing to the garish-coloured dyes used to produce the pattern. But it was in fair condition and the material warm. With another anguished glance into the backyard below, she turned her attention to finding needles, thread, and the small pair of scissors which were all they possessed.

"Better start before the afternoon light fades," she suggested, and Belle needed no further encouragement.

****

Chapter Four

It was almost by return of post that Hannah received replies from Mrs Mariah Simpson and the Reverend Lovatt-Browne delivered by a red-jacketed letter carrier whom she met as she was leaving the house. "And there's one for Mrs Mary Wilson at this address." Hannah returned indoors clutching the correspondence and leaving her landlady's mail on a small hall table, climbed the stairs.

"These are replies from both Mrs Simpson and the Reverend," she told her mother. "Let's see what they say."

The former wrote fulsomely, delighted to have heard from Hannah and to know that both she and her dear Mama were in fair health and had suitable lodgings. Hannah smiled grimly and wondered what her correspondent would say if she could see them now. "My dear," she continued," I have no hesitation in providing you with the best possible character reference. In the years that I have known you and your family, I found you to be honest, polite and diligent. You are helpful and kind...there, dear, it is the truth and I hope it will satisfy any potential employer, who may contact me directly, of course."

The Rector of Longwell came straight to the point; his written remarks aimed not at Hannah but at whoever might consider offering her employment.

"I have known Hannah Morley for many years and I am acquainted with one who tutored her, again for a substantial amount of time. I am informed that she attained a high standard in the following subjects, these being: arithmetic, written English and English history. My understanding is that she is proficient in watercolour painting, sewing and the playing of the pianoforte..."

His name was signed with a flourish: *Horatio Lovatt-Browne. B.D.*

Leaving her mother to her sewing, Hannah informed her that she intended walking to the workhouse with a view to discussing employment. "And don't worry about me. I assure you that armed with such references, I could become a governess in many a grand household. But I have no mind to do that, Mama. They are subservient, put-upon creatures belonging neither to upstairs nor down."

Walking briskly, she reached her destination within half an hour. The porter seemed to recognise her and on this occasion gave a crooked smile that revealed broken black stumps of teeth. As before, there was the unlocking of an outer door when she reached the main building and then she being ushered into the same drab office where some attempt had been made to create order. Again, she waited for Mrs Stannard to appear and when she did, the lady seemed agitated.

Hannah, having been told to seat herself, handed the letters across the expanse of an old wooden desktop. "I can see I have taken you away from your duties, so may I leave these with you and call again at a more convenient time."

"There is no convenient time in a place such as this. You will hear sooner or later because word gets out. Today a lunatic jumped from a third-floor window and died in the concrete yard below. We are in the process of repairing and replacing bars, but for this unfortunate soul, we were not in time. The building has been left to rot and the inhabitants with it. I feel in need of a strong cup of tea to restore myself. You may join me." She crossed to a bell pull and when a tall young woman wrapped around with a large grey apron answered the summons, requested that a tray of tea be brought. Hannah noticed that she smiled at the woman and when the tray appeared, thanked her graciously.

"We have started a programme whereby some of the young women are being trained for service. As you may know young girls, children no more, are sent to decent homes where one hopes they are treated well and receive training. But some girls have been here for years and my idea, of which the guardians approve I may say, is to try and train these older girls and get them out into the real world. Oh, dear, I am riding my hobby horse again!"

"It is a wonderful idea, Mrs Stannard. May I ask what other reforms are underway?"

"You may, but if I begin to tell you we shall be here all day!" She paused to reach into a cupboard for two china cups and began to pour thick brown liquid into them. "My goodness! This tea is so thick a mouse might tap dance on it! Now, your references. She spread the sheets of writing paper and bent over them. Mm...these people speak highly of you, Miss Morley. Since we last met, I have given thought to what we require and how you might fulfil the need. I mentioned previously that we will be engaging a teacher and an assistant. We have someone to oversee the girl's tuition and if you are interested in becoming her assistant, I will ask someone to show you the schoolrooms and tell you more about your duties."

"There is the question of my mother, Mrs Stannard. I cannot live in."

"Indeed not. I would expect you to arrive here no later than half past six in the morning because your day will begin with helping the small children wash and dress and take nourishment before the start of lessons. However, I go too fast. The guardians have to agree to most appointments and your application will be submitted to them." She halted to draw breath. "No less than three of the guardians must attend a meeting but this is a large Union and we shall have more than that present when they meet next week. Now, my dear," she rose to her feet, "you have to know what you are applying for and be shown around so I shall find our self-appointed housekeeper. There's a conundrum for you! There is no such position here but Agnes Blair, one of our inmates, believes differently. I think she was housekeeper to a rather grand family at one time and is still an efficient woman despite her weaknesses."

The woman proved to be a heavily built, sandy haired Scotswoman whose weight did not affect the speed with which she led Hannah on a tour of inspection. "Ye'll not see the whole place, dinnae think it. Ye could stay a week and not dae the rounds, but I'm to show ye the schoolrooms and I'll tell ye about the rest. There's aye some sad folks and that's a fact, and who should know better than auld Agnes." Then she brightened. "Youse are a pleasant looking lassie."

The schoolrooms were situated on an upper floor, the first overlooking what appeared to be a small graveyard. "Pauper's burial ground," was the explanation. "That's why there are the wee markers for some and nothing for others. For mysel' I dinnae think the bairns should be looking at such a gloomy place and mebbe it'll change, but this is what we have for the noo."

The room was large and cold but far from airy. The low ceiling proved claustrophobic. In a fireplace at one end burned a fire that threw out little heat and did not dispel the dampness. Hannah shivered. The walls were bare and a black chalkboard stood at the front beside a tall oak desk, presumably the teacher's. On every other desk was a writing slate.

"They tell me there'll aye be changes and they cannae come too soon. The bairns are always ill wi' coughs and sneezes and twa died of the pneumonia a week ago and Mr Gidley was fair upset. I heard that from Mrs Stannard. She's a guid women, that one. Aye, a guid woman."

"If I am engaged, will I be in this room?" asked Hannah. Agnes shook her head.

"Nay lass, not unless ye are to be top teacher! Ye'll be in the room across the passage, but to my mind it's the better o' the twa. I'll show ye before the bairns return from their midday meal."

The room was marginally brighter but the square windows were placed high in the walls and it left much to be desired. Hannah imagined pictures on the walls. "Have you met the 'top teacher' as you call her?"

"I have. Miss Phipps. I'm told she once taught the children of gentry. Say nae mair!"

"Then I shall not enquire but make up my own mind should we be working together."

"It'll nae be like that lass. Ye'll be working *for* the besom. Oh, dearie me. My tongue is an unruly member as the Good Book says. Tak nae heed."

"I shall forget you ever mentioned the lady," Hannah promised as they descended a wide stone staircase and she was rewarded with a broad smile. There came the clatter of utensils but no voices. As if Agnes Blair caught her thoughts, she said, "Nae speakin' at meal times. Things are changing with Mr

Gidley in charge but auld habits die hard, as they say, and the goings-on here were cruel, so they were. Here we are then."

They stood at the entrance to a hugely proportioned room. On one side and seated at long trestles were small boys, almost certainly all under eight years of age. On the other side and similarly seated were small pasty-faced girls. The boys sported close-cropped hair but the girls' heads were covered by navy blue caps and they were uniformly clad in navy serge which must have scratched and irritated delicate skin.

"Aye, weel, the food has improved wi' a new master and matron," Agnes Blair informed. "Meat twice weekly it is noo, bread baked in the basement kitchens and fruit in season. The wee souls won't know their born."

"That sounds a little too optimistic," Hannah said, her voice husky with emotion. "Haven't you noticed? Their eyes are dead."

"Aye, but at least these bairns are safe."

Were they? Hannah hoped so. Leary and Sal came to mind. As soon as Mama finished creating the tartan dress, she would take it next door and if there was enough leftover material, there might be one for Leary too.

"It will be a week or so before I hear anything from Mrs Stannard," Hannah informed her parent a day or so later. Belle frowned.

"I told you I do not wish you to find employment in *that place.*" *Mama could not bring herself to say the word,* thought Hannah. "With those references you could find something else, if you must."

"You know I must," Hannah said crossly. "We cannot live on air. Now I think of it, you could take in sewing. You are good with your needle and that dress is excellently made."

"I am not saying I will never do so but not whilst we live where we do. Who would come to this door and leave their alterations or orders? Their confidence would drain away as soon as they turned the street corner, and if by chance they arrived on the doorstep, Mrs Wilson would scare them away. There, that is the last stitch in the hem, thank goodness, for it is getting dark and my eyes are sore peering at tiny stitches. I had to finish with white thread as I had run out of red, but nobody will notice."

"I shall take it to the door as soon as we have eaten. We have new bread and not so new cheese," she laughed, "but it will do well enough. I shall make us a warming herbal tea. By the way, Mama, was poor little Sal in next door's backyard?"

"Not the child, but a young woman. I caught the merest glimpse and then she disappeared from view. Pale face, hair scratted back and she was wrapped around with a tartan shawl. That's why I noticed particularly, it was the tartan, you see. But I saw her only once. Not a servant, I would say, but who knows? Here, my dear, we will wrap the dress later. I am waiting for my tea."

An hour or two passed before Hannah went downstairs with the dress neatly parcelled in brown paper unearthed from the trunk which held a multiplicity of belongings and useful items. There was no sign of their landlady or of Leary, who seemed to spend most of her time hidden away in the scullery.

Dimly lit by fitful moonlight, the street outside seemed threatening in a way Hannah had not known when living in a village. On moonlit nights the cottages and fields had been illuminated and hid few secrets, and candles and oil lamps shone from cottage windows. Even on the darkest night and carrying a lantern, one had felt safe. Here, danger might lurk in any of the shadows and they were many as houses crowded together, yet despite their proximity, people seemed to scurry indoors and mind their own business. In this area nobody seemed to look to the needs of a neighbour. With swift steps she rounded the holly bushes and approached next door.

No sooner had she knocked on the door than it sprang open, revealing a long dark hall lit by flickering candles and a large oil lamp; its proportions were the mirror image of Mrs Wilson's, "You're late. You was expected five-ish, soon as it got dark. What you playin' at? We don't suffer fools gladly, so don't think it."

"It is me, Hannah Morley, from next door. We found something that might fit the little girl; Sal, isn't it?" She held out the parcel.

There was a momentary silence and then Hannah felt a hand push her in the ribs. "Don't you come sticking your nose in here. I was expectin' a friend. What's that you say? Somethin' for that little varmint? She don't need nothing. Still, seein' as you've gone to trouble…give it here, then get going. Like I say, we don't welcome strangers."

"I doubt you welcome anybody." The words slipped out before Hannah could stop them. "And if I *had* been a friend of yours, which God forbid, I'd have turned and walked away. Goodnight, whoever you are."

The door slammed in her face and with a fast beating heart, Hannah ran to Mrs Wilson's door which was till ajar. The sooner she was earning and they might move from this area, the better.

"It doesn't do to make enemies," Belle chided when she heard the story. "The woman sounds nasty and I can only hope the child is given the dress which was a labour of love."

"I know, and I am afraid if that horrible woman *is* angry with me, she will take it out on little Sal, and you're quite right, of course. She may never see the dress, leave alone wear it. Why are people so ghastly?"

Two days later, Hannah knew for certain that Sal would never wear the dress, for turning into a side street not a quarter of a mile from Blackfriar's Lane, there it was hanging in the front of the pawnbroker's window.

****

Chapter Five

There was no mistaking her mother's design and workmanship. The tartan material glowed amidst a sea of old boots, dusty jackets and faded skirts.

You bitch, that was for Sal. The words arose in her mind before she could stop them and somewhat relieved her feelings. The child had so little and was almost certainly badly treated and now all Belle's work and her own goodwill had been for nothing. On an impulse she entered the shop where a variety of odours assailed her, none of them pleasant. Becoming accustomed to the gloom, she saw a tall thin man behind a low counter which he grasped with a bony none-too-clean hand as if to steady himself.

"So what can I do for you, pretty lady?" His tone was wheedling as if he expected her to produce a case of jewels from which he might take his pick and recompense her as little as possible.

"You can tell me about the tartan dress in your window," she began and then modified her tone as he bridled. "I mean, it is charming and looks new. I may wish to buy it for my niece so should like to know where it came from."

Hooded eyes surveyed her, weighing her up and his chances along with it.

"It's a sad tale. The saddest. Bought by a mother for her daughter and now the woman left grieving and the dress unworn."

"May I examine the garment, please?"

A moment later Hannah found what she was looking for. A length of tiny white stitches along the hemline.

"I am not sure." She glanced at the broker, who was almost certainly under the influence of alcohol or possibly drugs of some kind or another. "I mean if it was meant for a child now deceased, it might be unlucky." Still, she thought, it might do for

Leary and so save her mother's eyesight sewing another dress in poor light. "How much is it?"

He mentioned an exorbitant sum and Hannah took a step backwards. *Really, she was a far better actress than she had ever imagined!* "I will pay half that amount or we have no agreement." From her reticule she produced a few coins and placed them on the counter.

"Two pence more and you can take the item." Hannah placed one penny next to the pile of coins and looked the man in the eye.

"My final offer," she said firmly and his fingers closed over the money. "Can you tell me who brought in the dress? You say she was a bereaved, poor soul, but what was her appearance?"

"What's that to you? You've got what you came for. How would I know any way? Folks come and go in this place."

"Mere feminine interest. My heart goes out to the woman. The dress is of good quality material so one can only assume she wished rid of it quickly because of its sad associations. A well-heeled person, maybe?"

"Like I said, I don't recall." His gaze flickered away from her own. "If that's all…"

It was obvious he was going to divulge nothing more and Hannah sighed as he bundled the dress into a parcel.

"I think I may know the lady in question. Tall and dark haired," she lied. "Rather an elegant creature."

"Nobody like that comes in here. More like a squat monkey, and a face like a plate." He laughed at what he considered to be his wit, followed Hannah to the door, and watched her as she walked away.

*****

"Mama, I am sure he spoke of that awful woman next door. You don't think Sal is really dead, do you?"

"She wasn't this afternoon. I saw the mite out there in the bitter cold. I confess I shed a tear and willed her to look up that I might wave to her, just to let her know she was not entirely alone in this world."

Hannah put an arm around her mother. "There's so little we can do. But if Mrs Wilson agrees, Leary may benefit. I shall take the dress downstairs this very minute. Say a little prayer that all goes well."

If her mother did as bidden, her prayer went unheard or was ignored. Tapping on the front parlour door, Hannah was told to enter the poorly lit room that was stuffed with oversized furniture. Her landlady rose from a fireside chair and her eyes widened when she saw the dress flung over Hannah's right arm.

"What's the meaning...? she began and Hannah hastened to explain.

"I...that is we, my mother and I, wondered if Leary might make use of this. We found it amongst our belongings." The lie tripped off her tongue. She was almost beginning to believe it.

Mrs Wilson crossed the wooden floor and snatched the dress, then eyed Hannah angrily.

"And what use would a scullery maid, a workhouse foundling at that, have for such finery? Answer me that, if you can. She is here to learn her place in the world which is to serve others. How would I discipline her if she spent half her time prancing about in that gaudy outfit? You astonish me, you do really, interfering busybody that you are." She flung the dress back at Hannah. "Take this thing and get back to your room. Oh, and let me tell you the dressing you applied to Leary's thumb didn't last two minutes."

"I daresay it became sodden. I can only hope there is no infection. Would you permit me to take a look?" She was certain the woman would refuse but instead she said grimly, "Very well. The child is no use to me whining that her hand hurts. You will find her in the kitchen."

"Where else would she be?" murmured Hannah sarcastically and knew she had been overheard as Mrs Wilson's mouth tightened.

As she made her way down a dark passage to the kitchen, there came a loud knocking at the front door and the murmur of voices. Then the front door slammed shut. It seemed that Mrs Wilson had been summoned away. Thank heavens for that.

Leary was the picture of misery and when Hannah sat beside her at the kitchen table, she realised that the child must be in excruciating pain. Her thumb was red and swollen, and candlelight showed that poison was spreading into her hand.

"Oh, you poor little thing. This needs a poultice. Let's see, what have we got? A bread or potato poultice might do."

"There's bread in the crock over there," whispered Leary, and Hannah reached inside and brought out half a loaf that was past its best. Reaching for a knife she cut off a good slice. "Now for a little milk and I shall need a pan. You will learn something if you watch me."

It took a while for the milk to heat on the stovetop and then Hannah placed the bread in it and mashed it to a pulpy mass. "Oh dear, we have no clean cloth. I must improvise." With that, she raised her skirts and ripped at the hem of her petticoat. "Beggars cannot choose, Leary."

Moments later, the poultice was applied to the child's hand and bound with strips of cotton material. "You must keep it dry. I shall tell Mrs Wilson the same and if needs be, I shall offer to do your work. You look tired, my dear. Where do you sleep?"

"In here. I gets the mattress out from under the cupboard and I settles on the floor. It's all right, miss. I keep fairly warm, but the stove is always out and dead cold by the early hours."

"I am leaving you but I shall be back with a written note for your mistress. It is very important that you do as I say or there will be trouble."

"You mean I might die?" Leary's tone was matter of fact. "I seen people die at the workhouse. Little 'uns. They was quite peaceful. Like they'd gone to sleep."

"I daresay, but peaceful or not *you* are not going to die." With that, she turned and went upstairs to return minutes later with a note for Mrs Wilson. "See this, I have offered to undertake duties that would cause you to wet that dressing. Tomorrow I shall examine the thumb and re-apply a poultice. No arguments; and Leary...I should like to call you something else when we are alone. If you could choose a name, what would it be?"

The little girl looked up at Hannah in astonishment and her cap fell off to reveal flattened hair that was black as pitch. *She's a little beauty,* Hannah thought.

"I don't know, miss. Never thought about it."

"Well, Leary is an Irish name so what about Kathleen or Rosaleen? Something like that?"

"I like the Rosa one. I can be Rosa when we are together. Is that what you're saying?"

"Indeed I am. Rosa is a pretty name for a pretty girl. Now time for bed. When will Mrs Wilson be back, I wonder? I shall leave this note on the table and I shall be down early in the morning to relieve you of duties that would endanger that thumb."

"She won't like it, miss. She'll call it interference and get mad."

"Then that is too bad, Rosa." She saw the shy smile and welcomed it. "I cannot say I am a match for Mrs Wilson, but I can be very determined."

"She'll get even, miss. She knows how."

*****

Hannah was as good as her word and appeared in the kitchen at six o'clock the next morning, a handful of linen dressings in her hand. Leary, already up and raking out ashes, greeted her with a wide smile and together they lighted the stove and set a kettle to boil.

"First things first, Rosa," and the child smiled, "I need to check your thumb and apply another poultice."

The thumb was no better but no worse either and that was a good sign, Hannah assured the child who was anxious that certain chores were completed before she took her mistress a cup of tea at seven on the dot.

When Mrs Wilson appeared, her face was wan and weary. "I saw your note," she greeted Hannah. "You say the thumb is poisoned. I suppose you know best and Lord knows we don't want a corpse on our hands."

"You won't have one. The wound must be kept dry, so with your permission I propose to wash the floors and prepare the vegetables if those chores would fall to R...I mean, Leary."

"As you wish." She then addressed the child. "I shall take my breakfast as usual in the back parlour. Hurry with it. I have to go out."

"She goes out a lot," remarked the child when they were alone and she was holding a piece of bread on a toasting fork to flickering flames. "Any old time and she's off. Good riddance, I say."

"I am sure you do, Rosa. She is sharp and unkind and unfeeling, but I sense that she has come down in the world and it is just possible that as you acquire skills and try to please her, your life may improve. Do you know what I am saying?"

"If I get quicker and she goes out more, we might rub along." She removed a piece of toasted bread and struck another slice on the fork.

"Something like that. Don't cross her. Here, I'll butter that and brew a pot of tea. You may carry in the tray as usual. See what a good team we make."

"I like you, miss. I wish you worked here too."

"I may not always be here. I am looking for work and may have found something and then I shall find other lodgings for my mother."

Rosa's little face fell. "That's terrible, miss. I don't want you to go."

"It's something I have to do but I promise to keep in touch with you." A thought crossed her mind. "Do you know or have you seen the little girl who lives next door in the house adjoining this one?" Was it naive to imagine the pair might become friendly?

"I dunno who lives there, miss. I never seen a girl. How old is she?"

"I am not sure. A bit younger than you. I saw her on one occasion and have caught the odd glimpse of her since."

"I don't know anyone, miss. Not since I left the work'ouse. I had a friend there but I expect she's gone somewhere else now. There, the tray's ready."

Hannah rattled through the work, leaving vegetables prepared and the stone floor scrubbed. For good measure she took a wet mop over the hall tiles and down the stairs. "I shall help you clear the ashes in the front parlour and lay the fire and after that I am sure you will manage by yourself. You know what I am going to say…"

"Keep that thumb dry!" Rosa almost shouted and they laughed together. It was good to see the child acting as a child should but her next words caused Hannah some concern.

"I think I love you," she said. Poor child, unloved and with nobody to love until now; but Hannah had plans to leave

Blackfriar's Lane. Was she doing more harm than good giving Rosa kindly attention?

****

Chapter Six

The letter offering her employment as an assistant teacher was brought to the door by a messenger from the workhouse.

"Mama, I am to present myself this very morning…" She scanned the official looking missive. "It is signed by Mr Gidley himself and he writes…let me see…*The Guardians have approved your application made in person to Mrs Stannard and have examined the letters containing your references. I have since contacted both Mrs Mariah Simpson and the Reverend Horatio Lovatt-Browne, and we are satisfied that you are suited to the position.* Isn't it exciting?"

"If you say so, my dear. But what hours are you expected to work? Will they pay you weekly or quarterly? And how much? And what about me, alone all day?"

"That concerns me, I admit. Could you perhaps tutor Rosa…you know, young Leary, when Mrs Wilson is absent? I could put it to her that the child would be kept out of mischief and might be more useful if she could read and write properly. And it won't be for long if I can help it. As soon as I receive pay, I shall look for other lodgings, that I promise."

Dressed in a sober grey woollen dress trimmed with blue ribbon that matched her bonnet and cloak, Hannah set out in good time for a mid-morning meeting. On the way she called into the apothecary's and whispered her good news to Sam who beamed. "It would be polite of me to inform your boss," she told him and was soon doing so.

His long nose quivered as usual but he seemed genuinely pleased to hear her news. "They say the Master is a new broom indeed, sweeping out every stinking corner and making free with public money, I shouldn't wonder. Still, something needed doing. That place had a bad reputation, very bad." He seemed on the point of saying more but his thin lips became a tight line. "Well, I wish you well, Miss Morley."

Feeling as if she had just taken her leave of friends, Hannah's steps were light as she hurried along busy pavements to the forbidding building that was to become her place of work.

"Wait here," she was told when she had explained her business to the same surly woman who had admitted her on her first visit. Moments later, she returned to lead Hannah along a wide stone-floored passage and paused before a battered door. "You're to see the Master." With that she turned and went away, leaving Hannah to knock on the door. This she did smartly, the confident sound belying her nervousness.

"Come along in." The voice was almost jovial and the appearance of the little man who rose from behind a wide desk littered with papers and ledgers fitted the friendly voice. Two other men, taller than he and prosperous looking, flanked him and they too rose to greet her. Mrs Stannard was seated behind them, close to a window that overlooked one of the exercise yards.

"Miss Morley, isn't it? Please be seated." He waved towards a most uncomfortable looking wooden chair that faced the desk. "Now, introductions. We know who you are and you have met our matron, Mrs Stannard, who tells me you impressed her with your manner and apparent abilities, but these gentlemen will be strangers to you. They are two of our guardians and when you came to their notice at our last meeting, expressed the wish to meet our new assistant teacher. Isn't that right, gentlemen? They have the power to engage or dismiss, you know!"

Mr Gidley...Mr John Gidley as Hannah was to discover, made it sound like a joke but she glanced rather nervously at his companions. Mrs Stannard looked amused, her glance indicating that the Master was a law unto himself.

"Let me introduce Mr Jasper Meredith." He turned to an immaculately dressed, handsome but severe faced man on his left, "and Dr Marcus Lisle is here on my right. These gentlemen may wish to ask you a few questions, Miss Morley, but be assured your position here is confirmed."

He is nice, she thought, *putting me at ease like this,* and she smiled at him.

Forty-five or thereabouts, her thoughts continued. *A bundle of energy.* She recalled old Alice, a supposed psychic who lived in Longwell. She swore she could see haloes and auras; some were dull whilst others pulsated with energy. If she had been present, Alice would doubtless see a lot of pulsation around Mr Gidley!

"Mr Meredith, you go first," invited the Master and that man seemed to strip Hannah with his gaze. It took all her self-control to fix him with a steady gaze.

"I am wondering, Miss Morley, why an attractive woman of your age, twenty, I believe, remains unmarried and seeking employment?"

Did she fancy Mrs Stannard's intake of breath or the frown that creased Mr Gidley's brow. Suppressing a flash of anger, she drew herself up. "I was engaged to be married when I was eighteen," she replied with coolness. "My fiancé had a change of heart when he met a plain faced-heiress. Obviously I was better off without such a man."

"Dear me, quite so, Miss Morley," put in John Gidley, looking disconcerted. "I believe your late father was a doctor of medicine, a country doctor, is that so?"

"He was clever and compassionate," Hannah said enthusiastically, "but impractical when it came to financial matters because he never refused to assist and advise even when he knew the patient could not pay. However, I am proud of him and so is my mother, even if we now find ourselves in straightened circumstances."

"Did you assist your father at any time?" The question was posed by Dr Lisle, a man in his early thirties, she estimated, less immaculately dressed than Mr Meredith but expensively so judging by the cut and quality of his dark suit. Black hair flopped over his forehead and his smile was friendly.

"Occasionally I accompanied him on visits and learnt how to bandage and poultice, and of course he talked to me about cures and medicines. He was fascinated by new modern cures and medicines but was also an advocate of natural country remedies, some of which are most effective, and free of course."

"Interesting," said the doctor, "but there is no money in hedgerow cures. However, your father seems to have been philanthropic and wise in the ways of his patients. Tell me, and I hope this does not sound too indelicate, did you assist in the care of new mothers and their babies?"

What an extraordinary interview this was proving to be!

"No, but I remember what my father said about babies that made a difficult entry into this world. He believed that mothers-to-be should watch their diet. He had noticed over the years that those whose diet was mainly fatty foods and bread had more trouble giving birth. The babies were large but not necessarily healthy." She paused and blushed at the strange turn of the conversation. "He advised a diet of lean meat and leafy vegetables when a woman is enceinte as she is more likely to produce a small healthy infant."

Mrs Stannard made a movement. "I think we should tell Miss Morley why we are pursuing this particular line of enquiry." She looked at Hannah. "You see, we are in need of decent women who can nurse or attend in the lying-in ward. Until now, some very unsuitable women, many of them inmates, have attended the sick and probably brought disease into the place rather than helped to eradicate it."

"I believed I was to teach, or at least assist in the classrooms."

"And so you are, lass." Mr Gidley reverted to a broad Yorkshire accent. "But we are under pressure and maybe you would you be willing to lend a hand in the sick wards? Not the itch or fever cases for we can't have thee taking lice or sickness back to your mother or spreading it amongst the school pupils, but you'd be right helpful in other ways; just until we appoint more staff."

"Yes, of course," Hannah replied decisively and Mr Gidley beamed.

"I knew it the moment I set eyes on you. I shall leave Mrs Stannard to acquaint you with your duties. Any other questions, gentlemen?"

"Just one." It was Mr Jasper Meredith who addressed her. "I believe you have lodgings in Blackfriar's Lane. Not the most salubrious area, is it?" However did he know? Maybe Mrs Simpson or the Reverend Lovatt-Browne had mentioned it.

"It's not what we are used to, but I shall find something better when I am able."

"Are you acquainted with your neighbours? Strangers in town may need a helping hand."

"I don't know any of the neighbours and our landlady does not encourage familiarity. I shall not miss Blackfriar's Lane." *I shall miss Rosa, though, and I shall worry about Sal next door.*

"We can arrange for your wages to be paid monthly although quarterly would be the usual thing," the Master was saying and she liked him even more.

"Monthly to begin with would be very helpful," she smiled gratefully. Then Mrs Stannard was indicating that they should leave the gentlemen and Dr Lisle was opening the door for them, and she and the other woman faced one another in the corridor outside.

"Men!" remarked the matron lifting her eyes heavenwards. "They ride their hobby horses whether it be a pretty face or medical cures! But I think you may be useful on the relieving ward and as we are in a state of flux and change just now, I think your schoolroom duties might be confined to the mornings and…oh, well, we shall see. Now, I propose that I leave you with Miss Phipps who is teaching the older girls. And tomorrow morning please report for duty as early as possible." She surveyed Hannah's dress. "I believed you to be in the later stages of mourning." Hannah explained and Mrs Stannard remarked that the late Dr Morley must have been an interesting parent to possess. "However, you look suitably attired to me. Miss Phipps may have other ideas. Don't say that I did not warn you. You'll find out."

Five minutes later, she entered the larger of the schoolrooms and came face-to-face with a woman possessing a most disagreeable countenance. Miss Phipps was nearing forty, her greying hair pulled back tightly. Dressed in unrelieved dark grey that did nothing for her sallow skin and with a sneer contorting her features, she looked, as Hannah's late father would have described her, unappealing. Fifty or so girls, wearing white aprons over their navy-blue serge, sat at tables ranged around the walls. It appeared that two girls shared every slate and Miss Phipps had been doing the rounds approving their work, or otherwise. The wooden ruler she grasped in her hand was raised ominously as if about to strike some unfortunate pupil.

"Well, come in and keep quiet," she threw at Hannah. "We are learning our sentences. I will deal with you later." *Deal with me!*

Later proved to be after an hour had passed and the girls were dismissed to take their midday meal. The tedium of that hour would long live with Hannah and she wondered how the girls, cold and frightened, had learnt anything at all. She wondered too how such a woman had come to be employed when it was obvious Mr Gidley was intent on making changes for the better.

"You will keep to the curriculum that I devise," Miss Phipps began. "The girls, that is both younger and older, learn the principles of arithmetic and the English language. They will be taught their Bible. I trust you are familiar with it and are a churchgoer yourself? I doubt, however, that many of them will be able to learn their Catechism but one can but try." She sighed heavily and moved close to Hannah who quite distinctly smelt stale perspiration. "I understand you will be living outwith the establishment." She sniffed. "That seems irregular to me but Mr Gidley has his own way of doing things." She made it sound like one of the seven deadly sins. "However, Miss Morley, I make the rules in the classrooms. You will dress soberly and control your wayward hair."

"Oh dear, is it wayward?" Hannah pushed back a strand of dark hair that had a habit of escaping her bonnet. "You will not sport dresses with colourful trims and frivolous tucks and fancy buttons. Do I make myself clear?"

"Indeed you do." Hannah knew she sounded sarcastic but could not help it. This woman seemed intent on making those around her miserable and ill at ease. How wretched *she* must be.

"I hope we may work together, Miss Morley, although I detect a rebellious spirit and I shall not tolerate it. Till tomorrow, then. I rise at five thirty to make my devotions and begin my daily duties at six thirty. You too will be in attendance at that time. Is that understood?"

Hannah murmured assent and took her leave. Whyever had such a repellent creature been appointed? It went against all she had learnt so far about changes for the better in this place. She could only suppose that Miss Phipps possessed excellent references and good teaching skills, but if that hour spent in the classroom was anything to go by, the latter were not in evidence today.

****

Chapter Seven

"…So, Mama, I shall have to leave Blackfriar's Lane no later than six in the morning and earlier if possible. I have spoken to Mrs Wilson about Rosa…now, do remember, Mrs Wilson calls her Leary…and I probably caught our landlady in a weak moment because she looked quite unlike herself, exhausted and anxious, but she has agreed that the child may sit with you on occasion and you may teach her sewing and reading. I suggested she would be of more use to her employer if she gained those skills."

"One could say that you are manipulative, Hannah, but I know you have acted in my best interests, and I daresay the child will benefit. I think, however, I shall continue to call her Leary or I may make a mistake over her name and give the game away, isn't that the expression?"

Next morning, Hannah crept downstairs to make her mother's breakfast and to check that Rosa's thumb continued to heal. She was wearing a brown dress that looked well on her, although she was unaware of that fact. Replacing shining brass buttons with ones of brown glass and having removed crocheted lace cuffs the dress was, in her opinion, quite spoilt. But it would not do to antagonise Miss Phipps on her first morning.

Wearing a black cloak belonging to Belle and a matching bonnet of her own, she crept to the front door where Rosa waited to see her depart. "I shall keep the old lady company." She referred to Belle and Hannah suppressed a laugh. Her mother was not yet forty-five years old! But, of course, to a child she probably seemed aged and her current poor health contributed to that image.

As always, it was dark in Blackfriar's Lane and she wished for municipal gas lighting and pools of brightness but steeled herself to walk through the back streets until she reached the lights of a wider thoroughfare.

It was as she stood outside the door drawing on winter mittens that she became aware of the sound of someone breathing heavily. Someone who stood on the other side of the dividing holly hedge. Someone who was either about to leave or enter the house next door. She had no desire to meet with any of the occupants except for Sal, so she stood and waited for whoever it was to make a move. After a couple of minutes came the sound of boots on the footpath and then the clack of them on the cobbled street, and she felt it safe to begin her journey.

She waited a full minute, then followed in the wake of the woman – surely those footsteps had belonged to a woman? Sure enough, as she turned a second corner and where gaslights flickered, she saw a female outline. A short dumpy figure carrying a large bag. Perhaps the woman sensed a watcher because she paused and glanced over her shoulder before disappearing between the houses, almost certainly down one of the narrow ginnels that led eventually to the stinking River Irwell that was filled with putrefaction and oily industrial waste from the factories and work yards that were strung along its banks.

Less than half an hour later, Hannah was being admitted to the workhouse that was filled with activity and subdued chatter at this early hour. Having been told to make her way to the girl's wards, she did so to discover the occupants washing and dressing themselves in the scratchy uniforms.

"Silence," Miss Phipps was bleating and her sharp tones had some effect because the children quietened, as did a couple of gossiping young assistants, and then, becoming aware of Hannah, they stared in fascination.

"I suggest you shed your outer garments, Miss Morley. You may leave them on the table over there and remove them later." She indicated a trestle type table that stood in the centre of the long dormitory. Her gaze wandered over Hannah but whether she approved or disapproved of the brown dress, it was impossible to know. "Now hurry up, prayers before we take our breakfast."

When ready, the children lined up, crocodile fashion, and were marched down wide stone stairs to the vast dining hall lit by large tallow candles that resided in wall-mounted wrought iron sconces, augmented by a few new gas lights that must surely soon replace the candles altogether.

On one side of the room, boys were already seated at long tables and the girls took their places on the other. Morning prayer consisted of Bible readings and prayers to Almighty God, thanking Him for delivering these children into the care of the workhouse where their souls might be saved even as their bodies were nourished. Miss Phipps led the extempore prayers, her voice rising in a pitch of fervour that failed to convince Hannah of her sincerity.

When she had finished what had seemed like a recitation, kitchen assistants placed platters of bread on each table and then returned to the kitchens for large pots of gruel, ladling the contents into bowls which were passed along the tables. There was no talking, no visible smiles or shared glances, and Hannah's heart was heavy.

Seated at one of the tables she supervised the smallest girls whilst taking sips of the gruel which she had to admit was thick and filling if lacking taste.

"For what we have just received…" intoned Miss Phipps at last, "may the Lord make us truly thankful." With one accord the children rose to their feet, formed long lines and filed from the room. Hannah followed the little girls, who led the way to their classroom.

"Have you got this clear? Arithmetic, English language, and then Bible study. You have forty girls aged between seven and ten years old, and you are here to teach them something. No mollycoddling, no gossiping, and be sure I shall check on your progress several times this morning, so be warned, Miss Morley."

"I shall do my best, Miss Phipps. I am sure the girls will show me where equipment is stored."

"Equipment? Oh, you mean slates. They are in the cupboard over there. Likewise the slate pencils. You have your own blackboard. Was there anything else, Miss Morley?"

Hannah surveyed the dreary room but shook her head. The windows were placed too high for the pupils to see the outside world. A few charts, maps and pictures would enliven the walls but there was no point in saying so.

The girls were docile and subdued, polite but unengaged, thought Hannah as she looked at her class.

"Now, you know my name but it will take me a while to get to know you all," she began. "So, for a start I suggest that if and when I ask any one of you a question, that person stands up and says her name loudly before giving me any other information. Is that clear? I am not going to fire questions at you but to begin with we are going to make a sentence about an animal. Who would like to suggest what animal that might be?"

There was no response. "Shall it be a cat or a dog, even a cow?"

A red-haired girl sitting to the front made a movement and Hannah smiled encouragingly. The tall child rose slowly, her pale cheeks reddening. "Noone," she whispered. "Me name's Noone."

"Have you another name? A Christian name?"

"Fran, miss. What about a cat, miss?"

"Thank you, Fran, a cat will do very well." She turned and wrote CAT on the blackboard. "Copy those letters, girls, and then we will construct a sentence that includes the word cat."

A few minutes later, Hannah did the rounds and helped those less able. "Now, what did the cat do? Let us construct a sentence that makes sense. For example we *could* write, 'The cat lay in the sun,' but I want you to make suggestions. You," she pointed to a wide-eyed child half way down the room, "what do you think the cat did? And please tell me your name first."

"Lottie. He got ate, miss."

"Do you mean the cat ate something?"

"No, miss. He was ate by a dog."

"Oh dear, I think we shall have to try again." Several girls sniggered before an extremely pretty fair-haired girl, taller and bolder than most of the others, stood up without invitation and said loudly, "Molly Tinsley, miss. How about: 'The cat sat on a wall'?"

Hannah wrote the sentence and watched as pencils squeaked and scratched the words on slate. The morning lessons passed remarkably quickly. Simple arithmetic followed. Dusters flapped as slates were cleaned but not before Hannah had inspected every one of them, correcting gently where necessary and speaking encouragingly. She fancied several of the girls were very poor learners. What her father would have described as slow on the uptake. Hannah was writing figures on the board when she was aware of a draught of cold air and turning saw that Miss Phipps stood in the doorway.

Her heart pattered uncomfortably although she had no need to be nervous. After all, the class was orderly and it was obvious that she was attending to her teaching duties conscientiously. Surely no fault could be found?

"I hope you remember no girl shall leave the room for any reason. They must learn to control their bodily functions until respite at noon, prior to the midday meal."

We shall all want to go now you have reminded us. Aloud she replied that yes, she understood. Unable to find fault, Miss Phipps smiled sourly and departed. The girls gave Hannah expectant glances as if she might make comment but she disappointed them.

By the time she undertook Bible studies, without the aid of the Good Book as there was no Bible in the schoolroom, Hannah was weary. She could not remember the full Catechism and come to that the entire Ten Commandments were rather hazy so she threw herself into the re-telling of the Stilling of the Storm as related by St Luke. As she possessed a natural talent for both story-telling and acting, the girls sat spellbound, their eyes wide with interest and so it was that Miss Phipps found them towards the end of the morning.

"Never in my life have I been more shocked, Miss Morley. What is the meaning of crashing around the room with flailing arms and making the sound of a roaring sea? This is sacred scripture and you are blaspheming. God will be affronted."

"He might be pleased the girls are interested and learning something in a new way." The words were out and there was no putting them back into her mouth.

"I shudder to imagine your eternal destiny, Miss Morley. You are a reprobate, a backslider and too full of yourself." Turning to the girls, she dismissed them before addressing Hannah again. "You and I are not finished. Not by a long way. I shall speak to you this afternoon."

"I am sorry, Miss Phipps, but I shall be otherwise engaged. I am part teaching assistant and part nurse. I think I am to report to the receiving ward to bandage, and things like that," she ended vaguely, unsure of what exactly she was expected to do.

"I heard you were a doctor's daughter. I knew you would be too big for your boots and no doubt you consider yourself better than anyone else." The woman looked as if she was about to spit blood or at the very least froth at the mouth.

"If that's the impression I have given, then I apologise. I have seen enough to know that nobody is better than anyone else. We all return to dust and ashes. My father used to say if the coffins of squire and labourer were opened two hundred years hence, nobody would be able to tell them apart."

"I have no interest whatsoever in what your father said or did. Whilst you are my assistant, you will teach in the manner I dictate. Failure on your part will result in serious complaint to the Board of Guardians. Understood?" Cold eyes raked her and Hannah quailed inwardly. Alice, the old woman of Longwell with all those psychic powers, would probably say that Miss Phipps had little positive energy and drained it from other people. *I bet her aura is purple or black!*

****

Chapter Eight

"The infirmary is across the yards, a big building. The main wards are upstairs, the receiving ward down. I warn you, the place stinks. One requires a tough stomach," Mrs Stannard told her. "But I am sure you will be worth your weight in gold." Her friendly tone was particularly cheering after that of Miss Phipps.

Hannah smelt the place before she entered a low-ceilinged room packed with humanity, most of it unwashed. Later she learned that one ill-functioning privy was situated off the room in a far corner. A couple of rough looking women tended some who waited for more expert attention; one held a sick bowl under the nose of a heaving woman and another mopped the floor in dilatory fashion.

"We have plans to improve conditions I am thankful to say. These patients are off the streets or on day relief – that means do not stay under our roof. Those who require to be admitted will be taken in if possible, but we are packed to capacity just now owing in part to the closure of areas for alterations. Annie…" she accosted the woman brandishing the floor mop, "I need jugs of hot water and bowls. Bandages I have in my bag, salves and ointments too."

The woman called Annie walked as slowly as possible to the door as if in protest. "I am afraid she is a difficult creature. Both these assistants are inmates. Oh, how I wish we might have women trained to nurse the sick. Mr Gidley believes the day will come, but one wonders. Now let us see where to start. That boy with the crushed finger, maybe."

She led Hannah to a boy of about twelve, his face drained of colour and his eyes fearful. "Let us look at your injury," she ordered, not unkindly, and he held out a filthy hand. One finger looked as if it had burst and was bleeding copiously. "Do you know how to deal with such an injury, Miss Morley?"

"I suggest the site is cleaned and a pad applied to the finger which is then bandaged tightly. The wound must be kept dry and examined daily."

"And to prevent infection? Well, you shall see what I have in my bag."

For the next two hours, Hannah was almost oblivious to her surroundings as she cleaned and bandaged, examined injuries and listened to Mrs Stannard's advice. The woman seemed to have a depth of experience and eventually she explained.

"My late husband was a doctor as was your father. We often worked together. He discussed his cases with me and we set up a surgery in the poorest part of York. He was an acquaintance of Mr Gidley who, when appointed Master here, suggested I apply for position as Matron. Like yourself, I am required to earn my living." She paused to look around at the remaining patients. "Miss Morley, there are at least five people here who should be admitted. For a start, the man with an infected foot that has poisoned his leg and that poor girl who is about to give birth and came in off the streets. I will leave you whilst I arrange matters."

Five minutes later whilst dealing with a leg scraped almost to the bone, Hannah looked up to see a familiar figure enter the foul-smelling room. "Dr Lisle, what a surprise!"

"It should not be. Today I wear my medical officer's hat. Yesterday I wore that of guardian. What have we here? You are doing a good job, Miss Morley. This wound, almost certainly industrial, will need much attention and will take a while to heal." He addressed the patient. "What is your occupation, my man?"

"Stone breaker, Here at the 'ouse."

Dr Lisle shook his head. "I doubt it is possible to rest it but the wound is severe and needs time to heal."

"Can't be done, sir Family to feed." The man winced with pain. "Gorra keep going."

"That's the trouble, isn't it? Pressure on all sides. Too little money, no security and large families; no education so no chance of getting out of a system that oppresses the poor." He seemed to be addressing the room at large but then turned his attention towards Hannah. "I am not a great philanthropist but believe me I have it in me to be a reformer. There is much to be done in this city and one or two affluent families are taking a lead, the Leighs, for example. You've heard of them, I suppose."

"No, but there is a great deal to be done everywhere," Hannah cleaned the wound and the man groaned. "I knew of widowed women and their families turned out of miserable cottages that had been their homes for years because the wealthy landowner wanted to re-let. Once as many as nine people, a mother and her children, ended in a workhouse."

"You and I must put the world to rights or at least discuss its wrongs," he smiled and pushed back dark hair, then seemed to remember the injured man. "Keep the wound clean and well padded. Get your wife to dress it and rest the leg at every opportunity."

"God bless you, sir, and the lady."

"He means you," whispered Dr Lisle and smiled when Hannah remarked that she had never felt less ladylike. Her dress was blood-stained, her hands sticky with ointment and her hair fast falling down. "Oh, you will do," was his remark before he turned his attention towards the woman who moaned and writhed as labour pains gripped.

At the end of a twelve-hour day, Hannah was free to leave. Outside the world was shrouded in thick sulphurous fog that lay like a suffocating blanket. Sounds were muffled and the light of flickering gas lamps, overdue for replacement mantles, barely penetrated the darkness and fog.

Pulling her cloak closely around her tired body and covering her mouth, she walked slowly back to Belle and another set of duties. There were few people about and those she passed edged away as she did herself, fearful of what the fog might conceal.

Twice she believed she had lost her way and panic rose, but having passed the apothecary's, confidence returned. It was short-lived because having left the main thoroughfare and turning into side streets, she became hopelessly confused. It was impossible to be sure that Blackfrairs Lane lay ahead. Putting out a hand to feel for brickwork or fence, she crept along slowly determining that if all else failed she would knock on a door and hope to receive directions. Then somewhere a horse neighed and her spirits lifted. The animal would not be unattended in this area. Help may be at hand.

Hannah realised two things simultaneously. One was that she was already in Blackfriars Lane and the other that the horse was close by. In fact, the thought had no sooner registered than she almost bumped into a vehicle drawn close to the footpath at the side of the street. Voices, an undertone of urgency and annoyance, the horse's hooves stamping on the cobbles and an indefinable sense of menace caused her to halt. She backed away, thankful now for the cover of darkness and fog.

"Get her in then. Go on, lift her up." It was a man's voice, surely, but muffled so she could not be absolutely certain. Well-spoken anyway. There seemed the movement of two or three people and she stepped back another few paces. "Get a move on, there. No time to waste and she'll not know."

Then the small drama was over. Words were exchanged and surely that was the clink of coins, the cab door was closed, and there came the crack of a whip. The vehicle creaked as it moved away. Hannah stood for a moment, alert and listening intently before edging along the footpath. Then through her knitted mittens she felt the prick of holly. Why! The horse and cab must have been outside number fourteen, Mrs Wilson's house, or the adjoining property.

Upstairs her mother fussed and exclaimed over her lateness. "My dear, I knew it was a bad idea. Working in *that* place and having to walk back in adverse conditions. This frightful fog came down before darkness fell and I have been worried out of my mind."

"Never mind that, Mama. I think it possible someone has been taken ill next door. Believe it or not there was a horse and cab outside as I came down Blackfriars Lane. I almost bumped into it. How they found their way in this fog beats me."

"I do hope it is not that child you call Sal." In the poor candle light that lit part of the attic room, leaving shadowy corners, Hannah saw her mother's worried expression. "Leary came up here two or three times for short spells and we looked from the window into next door's yard. That little creature was out there for hours, clutching some thin garment around her and weeping. I am sure of it because she wiped her face often. I watched until the fog descended and she was *still* outside."

"It is outrageous; such cruelty, and an unjust punishment if that's what is was. Maybe she *has* been taken ill. I wouldn't be surprised if she developed pneumonia." She paused having taken off her cloak and bonnet. "I shall tell you about my day later. Have you eaten, Mama?"

Belle nodded. "Leary has taken me under her small wing. Broth that was fairly tasty and bread that nearly pulled out my teeth!" Hannah was pleased that her mother seemed in better spirits and able to make a small joke. "I shall teach her letters and devise simple sums. She will be quick to learn, in my opinion. Do you not find it surprising that Mrs Wilson should permit her visits?"

"I do, Mama, but she seems abstracted. It's almost as if she has too much on her mind to care one way or another. Or perhaps she is unwell and sickening for something. There are debilitating winter ailments doing the rounds." Hannah was opening the large trunk that held most of their belongings. "I need another dress. This one shall be for the hours spent nursing because it is already stained, and I shall require another, plain and suitable for when I take a class of girls."

Over the next few days, Hannah became used to an almost unvarying routine. Rising early, she attended to Belle and tidied the attic room. Then she walked to the workhouse in darkness, hurrying as did the factory workers, droves of them, although many others would have started their day's work even earlier. Then began days so busy that her head spun.

Miss Phipps and her intrusive observation of activities in Hannah's orderly class was a source of huge irritation and some anxiety. Hannah dared not disobey and act out Bible stories, or tales from history, for fear of retribution, but she tried to involve the girls in the learning process and taught them several poems and verses. 'Lucy Gray' was a firm favourite.

"It was first published over fifty years ago," she told her class. "I don't expect you to remember that fact...well, not all of you, but see if you can all learn some of the verses. It's a good thing to have a brain that is a store-house full of interesting things."

Did she imagine increased interest? The girls were so cowed anyway, so lacking in initiative, their young spirits crushed, but there were a few pairs of bright eyes and when they recited together, their voices rose and fell as if the words held some meaning.

"So, and what are you learning today?" Miss Phipps had appeared and ignoring Hannah stood with folded hands, long pale fingers pressed together, waiting for an answer.

It was Molly Tinsley who stood up, her short fair curls haloed around her small dainty head. "Please Miss Phipps, we were learning about Lucy Gray. You know, the poor girl whose ghost came back."

"What utter nonsense! For the sake of all that's Holy, what are you teaching them, Miss Morley?"

Hannah felt anger rip through her. *Careful, don't let her know she has upset you.*

"Oh dear, Miss Phipps. Molly did not explain very well. You will recall William Wordsworth's moving account of the child lost in a snowstorm on the moor. The poem first appeared in a publication called Lyrical Ballads in 1800 or thereabouts. I think the volume contained work by Samuel Taylor Coleridge as well."

"That's quite enough from you," her superior said rudely. "There's no need to show off your knowledge and in any case you would do better to teach these ignorant children poetry of a religious nature. Do you understand?"

"Indeed we do, don't we, girls?" Hannah could not resist, and encouraged, most of her pupils chorused, "Yes, Miss Phipps."

Of course she would pay for it later but the expression on the other woman's face was a study to behold and well worth it.

Later she found herself recounting the incident to Mrs Stannard as they sat over bowls of mutton broth at a top table in the dining hall. "Oh, do be careful, Miss Morley. It does not do to make enemies. I rather think Miss Phipps has friends in high places. At one time she was employed by a wealthy local family, cousins or friends, I am not sure which, of one of our guardians. You have met him, of course, Mr Jasper Meredith."

The next morning Molly Tinsley was absent from class and Hannah asked if anyone knew why that should be? Red-haired Fran Noone stood up and said timidly, "We think she's moved in with Miss Phipps, miss. She went yesterday afternoon when we were doing needlework. She was fetched."

"Wait here quietly, girls. I need to investigate. Don't make a sound."

The injunction was unnecessary because the children lived in fear of being punished for any misdemeanour.

After rapping on the other classroom door and being told to enter, Hannah did so and faced a fierce looking tyrant. "May I have a word, Miss Phipps?" She did not wait to be told that this was not the moment, instead she rushed in with her question: "Molly Tinsley is absent from my class. I am informed that she has been moved up into your own."

"What I decide to do in the best interests of my pupils, *mine* I remind you, is entirely my affair. Tinsley may be younger than others in my class but she will fit in very well. A bright pupil. Has that answered your impertinent question?"

"Yes, thank you, Miss Phipps." The words almost stuck in Hannah's throat as she scanned the rows of girls looking for a halo of golden hair. Yes, there was Molly, smirking in a self-satisfied manner from her seat at a table placed against the bare wall. Hannah nodded in her direction and took her leave. *I shall get even with you, Miss Phipps.*

The opportunity arose sooner than anticipated when once again she sat beside Mrs Stannard at the midday meal. "I have been thinking about the classrooms," she said as she cut into gristly meat. "It is not a subject I am in a position to raise with Mr Gidley but I feel the pupils would benefit from charts and maps, maybe some pictures. I have a Bible full of beautiful pictures and something along the same lines but larger would look well."

"Do I sense more than a simple suggestion, Miss Morley? Never mind, I am in agreement and will raise the matter with the Master. He is keen that young minds are filled with readily absorbed information, that colour is brought into drab lives. He used to teach in one of the ragged schools, you know."

"I am afraid I don't know much about them."

"In a nutshell, Miss Morley, the children who attend are too poorly clad and unwashed to attend Sunday schools, cannot afford to pay for education, and are usually from city slums. People such as Mr Gidley offer lessons in the evenings and on Sundays too. He firmly believes that education is a necessary aid to upward social mobility." Her tone was warm and enthusiastic. "It is an enormous privilege to work with such a man as you will discover for yourself."

61

A week later, Hannah did indeed discover when boxes arrived in the classrooms, filled to the brim with the very items she had mentioned to Mrs Stannard, who herself appeared on the scene just as Miss Phipps looked about to become a victim of spontaneous combustion, as Hannah later related to Belle.

"The Master's idea, Miss Phipps. As you know, he is keen that young minds are fed. As far as I know, and with the full approval of our guardians, naturally, he has purchased maps and charts and some suitable pictures. See! Here is a lovely framed depiction of Ruth gleaning in the fields. Such a wonderful Old Testament story, I always think."

Hannah was thrilled with the contents of the box that arrived in *her* classroom with assurances that by the morrow all would be hung on the walls. "Come girls," she invited, "this is wonderful. See what we have here!"

There were murmurs of anticipation and excitement as the children gazed at maps that were incomprehensible to them, a wall calendar, and large framed pictures of New Testament scenes; the Feeding of the Five Thousand, Christ blessing the children and the Raising of Lazarus.

"I know that one, miss," chanted Fran Noone. "He came back from the dead, but he wasn't a ghost like Lucy Gray. That's right, in't it, miss?"

A little of Hannah's pleasure drained away when she met with Miss Phipps at the end of the morning session. "I don't know how you did it, Miss Morley, but I know full well you are at the bottom of all this."

"All what?" replied Hannah innocently, guessing what was coming next.

"This…well not exactly rubbish, but ornamentation to hang on our walls. These children will be spoilt; they will expect more of life than it can possibly offer them. You have a lot to learn, young woman."

Hannah's cheeks blushed and as usual when confronted by this unlikeable woman, her heart beat faster, but she was not going to show her emotions.

"I cannot argue with Mr Gidley. My understanding is that he believes children should *enjoy* learning and will benefit from educational aids."

"Is that what you call them?"

"No, Miss Phipps. It is what Mr Gidley calls them or so I have heard. Besides, we all need a little colour in our lives." She did not mean to run her gaze over the unbecoming, unadorned, charcoal grey dress worn by the other woman, and chided herself for what amounted to unkindness, but she had been unable to prevent herself. Confused and alarmed that she, Hannah Morley, possessed a streak of cruelty, she softened her words by adding wistfully that speaking for herself she often longed for colour.

Before she changed and made her way to the infirmary and the duties that awaited, she caught sight of Miss Phipps again. It was towards the end of the midday meal, referred to as dinner, and the woman was standing over Molly Tinsley. To Hannah's astonishment, Miss Phipps was running her fingers through the child's fair hair, almost as if she was playing with the golden strands.

Well, maybe Miss Phipps harboured a secret and unnatural predilection for pretty little girls. Hannah had heard tell of such things. There had been a sad middle-aged woman in Longwell who had tried to entice the young girls into her cottage, and there had followed whisperings and rumours of her furtive fondling. She had become a laughing stock and a pariah. *"Make sure you run past her cottage,"* or *"Got yer chastity belt on, lass?"*

There was nothing she could do about it, Hannah told herself. Perhaps, though, she had misinterpreted the action. Perhaps Miss Phipps had been caught in a moment of rare kindness.

The infirmary teemed with those unable to pay for medical services. As Mrs Stannard explained, "These folk had been turned away from the voluntary hospitals and were too poor to go elsewhere, jobless and often homeless." She added that the service she and her assistants provided was practically unfunded and although Dr Lisle received remuneration for attending those on Outdoor Relief, that is those sick who received monies from the Union, and for his attendance upon those in the wards, he had to pay for prescribed medicines himself and his visits were seldom more frequent than once weekly.

"What happened to the woman in labour yesterday? Hannah wanted to know. "Did she give birth safely?"

"She gave birth to a live female child, a poor mite but likely to survive. But a sad ending, the mother overlaid the child this morning.

"You mean she killed the child by lying on top of it?" Hannah was aghast.

"We could not prove it was intended. It happens quite often. I was called to the woman at five this morning when it was discovered. The mother seemed unmoved, relieved of a burden, no doubt. Well, if she makes her living on the streets as is likely, how could she cope with a baby in tow? She could not afford to pay for its care and perhaps there was nobody with whom to leave it. Perhaps she did her child a favour."

"You can't mean that, Mrs Stannard. That is quite dreadful. She killed her baby to save it from future misery? Is that what you are saying?"

"It's possible, but I doubt the poor girl thought of that. She may have been temporarily deranged following the birth or it may have been accidental, although I think it unlikely. I suspect she felt trapped by circumstances completely outwith her control and it was one less burden to carry."

Hannah felt tears pricking behind her eyelids and fought to control herself. She would never be able to remain calm in such a situation, she was sure. Of course, Mrs Stannard had seen much more of the world and its misery, but even so, what she had just heard was unbearably sad and distressing. "Come along, Miss Morley…Hannah…we have work to do. Focus on that and think too of the transformation that will take place in the classrooms. I would say that we achieved a victory of sorts in that department, wouldn't you?"

****

Chapter Nine

"I am not expected to work on a Sunday, Mama, but I am expected to attend Divine service. The Master, Mr Gidley, knows that I belong to the established church so I may attend locally. On the other hand, there are services at Bronton on both Sunday mornings and afternoons when, as Mrs Stannard puts it, 'the chaplain attends to the spiritual needs of the inmates.' One could say he has a captive audience."

Her mother looked up from the alterations she was making to a dress of her own so it might fit Hannah. "You sound acerbic, my dear, a trifle disillusioned, if I may say so. Does that place have a chapel or place of worship?"

"Not yet, but there will be one when the new building programme is completed. At present the services take place in the dining hall. Do you think I should attend?"

"Perhaps, dear, until we are more settled and then we will probably go to the established church closest to our home. I so miss Longwell and our dear old church there."

"Mr Gidley is non-conformist, a Baptist I think, no, Methodist…oh, I am not sure, but I don't gain the impression that he minds how his staff label themselves as long as we try to do our best and treat other people with respect and what he would call Christian kindness."

"Admirable," commented Belle, snipping at a thread. "You say he is a bundle of energy."

"I don't see much of him at all, but Mrs Stannard tells me of his innovations and plans, and she saw what he had written in the Day Book. He keeps a record of absolutely everything, Mama. The names of every single person who enters the workhouse even if they stay for one or two nights. He writes their details and of their circumstances…some are desperately sad…such as the woman and child sleeping in a hedge." She sighed and bit her lip. "He records the names of runaways and punishments and even mentions purchases. Here is what she said he wrote, and I have to agree that it shows a degree of tenderness, because he recorded having ordered *'comfortable cots for the little children.'* Oh, and he is suggesting to the Guardians that some form of Christmas entertainment is arranged for them. For the children, that is."

"My goodness! He will be proposing that a tree be brought inside and decorated. It is becoming the custom and rather charming, if outlandish."

"I don't imagine Mrs Wilson will indulge in such frivolity but we might have our own tiny little tree, and we could hang biscuits and sweets from the branches. Rosa, that is Leary as you know her, would love it. Did she visit you today?"

"We were well into our lessons when there was such a to-do next door, such screaming and yelling, and the child fled. Later, when she reappeared, she was upset about something else. Apparently, Mrs Wilson had a male visitor and Leary took tea into them. She was disturbed by the way he looked at her and that she was asked to turn around that he might see her better. Oh, and he asked her to remove her cap and commented on her hair. My dear, how old did you say she is?

Hannah tried to remember. "I think she had been told she was about nine or ten. Why, Mama?"

"I am sure she must be older. Her figure is beginning to change; you know, assuming more female contours."

"Oh, you mean she is developing breasts."

"There is no need to be coarse, Hannah. But I suppose so. She was standing beside the window and as she turned her dress pulled across her chest and I couldn't help noticing. I wondered whether she might be closer to eleven or twelve."

"What you say is very concerning, Mama. Keep an eye on her. You are the only one to do it because I am away for hours every day."

"I am not sure I am up to the responsibility. All I can do is ask and listen. Oh, how I hate this place; the noises coming from next door and that poor child out in all weathers, the mice in the walls and our horrible landlady. Life can be very grim, can't it?" *Far worse than you can ever imagine.* Hannah thought of the street girl who had smothered her new-born baby. She would not tell Mama about it or about some of the other things she had seen and heard. Instead, she described the boxes that had arrived in the classrooms and Miss Phipp's reaction.

*****

Hannah attended the afternoon service at the workhouse and was secretly amused by the wording painted on banners that had been hung on the bare walls of the dining hall. *"The Lord is merciful,"* she read, and another, *"God is a very present help in times of trouble."*

Mrs Stannard appeared at her side. "The problem is that God works through human hands and they are often less than kind! I thank Him daily for Mr Gidley because he *is* compassionate." She glanced round at the people present. "How many of these have cause to be grateful for anything?

Suffering was etched on the faces of the destitute surrounding her and Hannah, always finding it difficult to look into eyes that were dull or pain-filled, certainly devoid of hope, looked down at the prayer book she had brought with her.

"You will not be needing that," Mrs Stannard whispered. "We have no appointed chaplain. So far the guardians have resisted the request for his salary. We have visiting lay preachers and a curate from a local parish comes here often. His sermons are short and to the point, full of anecdotes and interest. There is no shuffling and not much sniffing and coughing when young Mr Christie is on duty as he is today."

"Inmates may attend local churches, mayn't they?"

"Oh yes, and they are bound to return to us immediately afterwards. Any who cause trouble in the town or are caught begging are compelled to miss a meal, but Sunday is a meat day so that is not too much of a problem. Come, let us take our seats."

'Young' Mr Christie was not quite as youthful as Hannah had expected. He was probably in his late thirties but possessed a full head of brown hair and a smile that embraced his congregation, or should that be audience, she wondered as a service such as she had never before attended, took place.

Mr Christie's prayers were short and to the point. If Hannah had been prepared for exhortations to be thankful and grateful, they were not forthcoming. As expected, a blessing was called down upon the beloved Queen and her family, and then for

Divine help in difficult and tragic situations, about which many of those present were obviously familiar. She suspected this dynamic man was approved of sincerely by Mr Gidley, but glancing around she failed to see him.

When the curate addressed the company the sufferings of Saint Paul imprisoned in Rome were interspersed with interesting glimpses into Mr Christie's own prison visiting. Then to Hannah's astonishment, he produced a flute with which to accompany the singing of a hymn.

It seemed that many present were already familiar with the words and Hannah blinked back a tear as cracked voices sang of "grace enough for thousands", and one verse made a huge impression upon her. Was Mr Christie covertly criticising those who imposed their will upon others? Miss Phipps came to mind as they sang:

"For we make His love too narrow
By false limits of our own.
And we magnify His strictness
With a zeal He will not own."

Later, Hannah was to meet Mr James Christie because Mrs Stannard announced that the curate always stayed for a cup of tea and she was inviting Hannah and a few other staff members present at the service to join them in Mr Gidley's office. Miss Phipps, she informed, would not be present as she had a free afternoon and was visiting friends, and for this Hannah sent up a fervent prayer of thanks although it would have been interesting to know what her protagonist thought of the words they had just sung.

Extra chairs had been brought into the large office and a log fire burned in the hearth. Two young girls brought in trays of tea and buns, and Hannah found herself seated between Mr Christie and a small middle-aged Welshman who announced that he was from Ruthin where he had a wife and two daughters. "Williams," he said, "Elias Williams, I 'ave been appointed tailor here." His accent was quite delightful with a rising cadence at the end of some words and every sentence. "Better pay here, you see. Dilys, my wife, that is, and our girls understand they'll not see much of me, but there'll be food on the table. Dilys ails, never strong, and it's Bethan, our eldest, who runs the house."

"I suppose the new train service has opened up possibilities of working distances further away from home…I have seen the splendid Victoria locomotive station… but you won't get back to Ruthin often, will you?"

"No, indeed. A few days now and then if I save up my free time. Mr Gidley is very understanding. Not here, is he, although we are making free in his office. I am told he still has a connection with one of the ragged schools. Could be there now. A good man, very sound."

"Miss Morley, I believe…" Mr Christie, who was battling with a sticky bun and a recalcitrant teacup that was in danger of falling on the wooden floor, was addressing her, and smiling kindly at the Welshman she turned to the curate. "May I suggest I hold the teacup whilst you tackle the bun?"

He grinned and looked boyish. "I see you come straight to the point," he said.

"To save *you* embarrassment and my skirt from being tea stained. My mother finished sewing this dress last evening."

Soon his gentle probing questions had elicited much of her situation and in response he informed her that his father had been a harness maker and his education undertaken by the local squire whose son he had saved from drowning when both boys had been ten years old. "It wasn't in these parts," he added, "but I find myself here because I felt drawn to city life, to the needs of people who have nothing and nobody to turn to. I suppose London might have absorbed my energies but I had no wish to travel so far south."

Hannah's mind was reeling with information and impressions by the time she started for home and Belle. Besides Mr Elias Williams and the Reverend Christie, she had been introduced to a serious young woman who was to take charge of the infant's nursery and another who was to assist Mrs Agnes Blair, the self-appointed housekeeper with what that woman considered to be onerous duties. It seemed that a large number of new staff were being recruited owing to the enlargement, rebuilding and renovations taking place.

There was so much to tell Mama and all of it quite fascinating, but first she must navigate streets that were once again shrouded in fog.

Rosa, or Leary, as her mother insisted on calling the girl, had appeared on one occasion only, her mother informed, and had been quite distracted because *that man* as she referred to him, had come calling again. She, Leary, had opened the door to admit him and he had brushed past her in a very familiar manner.

"It seems he pushed against her and as she turned to close the door, he fondled her...well, you know..."

"I can guess. It sounds outrageous, but perhaps she was mistaken, already in a nervous state seeing him again."

"I don't think so, dear. She said he grabbed her nether regions."

"You mean her buttocks, Mama."

"That is not how *she* referred to those parts, but I guessed it to be so. Most worrying is that Mrs Wilson was present. At least, when Leary turned around the woman was standing in the hallway, calmly I gather, as if nothing amiss had occurred."

"It's worrying. The child is in danger, Mama, I am sure, but I am at a loss to know what to do."

Next morning the fog still drifted around the back streets but not quite so densely as the previous evening and when Hannah took the now familiar walk to work and turned from Blackfriar's Lane into a cutting that joined the main road, she glimpsed ahead the same squat figure she had spied days ago and once again carrying a large bag. As if aware that she was being followed, or perhaps whoever it was had heard the clack of boots on cobbles, the figure seemed to put on speed and disappeared between the houses.

Delivering laundered clothes or dressmaking alterations? Hannah put speculation aside as she drew close to the apothecary's where Sam Webster was already at his work counter, candles burning brightly as he mixed and pounded ingredients. Not yet open to the public he nevertheless crossed to the door and greeted Hannah as he opened it.

"Life treating you well, I hope, Miss Morley? She nodded smilingly and hoped he too was in fine fettle.

"Mustn't grumble. Except for the hours. The old man expects me to work late every night whilst he scuttles home at

70

six o'clock. I might as well sleep under the counter. It'd save time!"

At the workhouse there was what her father would have referred to as "a bit of an uproar."

"We aye see dreadful things and hear of more," Agnes Blair greeted her. "There was that wee new-born bairn found dead in the stinkin' Irwell, but oh, the wickedness of this makes my puir heart fail."

"What's happened, Mrs Blair? Tell me, do."

"Whit's happened she asks! Only a puir wee lass found wi' her throat cut and she still trying to breathe. It'll be a mercy when the bairn passes, so it will. Whatever divil did the deed and left her no doot thought she was away to the angels. But the Lord had different ideas."

Of course, she should go straight to the classroom but Hannah's footsteps marched towards the infirmary. After all, some of her duties lay in that direction. Passing through the outer ward where the casuals gathered for attention and possible admittance, she began to climb the wide stone stairs and was met half way by Mrs Stannard who was coming down.

"You have heard," the woman said simply. "It is just a matter of time before the girl dies. Loss of blood and shock, not to mention exposure to the elements. God knows how long she had been lying in that foul place."

"Where?" asked Hannah, followed quickly by, "Is there anything I can do?"

"You might sit with her awhile and it will not be for long, believe me. I will send word to Miss Phipps and she can make the best of it. The child is in a side ward. As to where she was found, on rough land close to the Chorlton Road, a haunt of vagrants and bad sorts, I believe. I await a police constable but it's no use, the child is long past speech."

Two minutes later Hannah stood in a small bare room gazing down at a still figure that might have been made of wax, but with blood matting fair hair and staining thick bandages that hid the neck wounds that drained her life. A none too clean sheet covered her body.

She stepped closer and reached for a hand that had escaped the sheet and hung limp and pale. Would the dying girl know she was not alone? She hoped so. Then her heart began hammering and letting go of the small hand with its dirt-encrusted nails she staggered slightly, nausea threatening as she took a closer look at the once pretty face.

It was Sal, she was as sure as she could be. Sal, the little girl who spent long cold hours in the backyard next door to number fourteen.

****

Chapter Ten

"Miss Morley, I should not have exposed you to this! At times I forget your youth. Sit down before you faint." Mrs Stannard was back and pulling forward an old wooden chair. "Such a dreadful thing to happen to a defenceless child. A maniac, a monster must have done this to her. I fear she is slipping away now, God rest her. Come, you take one of her hands and I will hold the other. There, child, there, may the Lord receive your spirit," she intoned softly and blinked back tears.

Hannah was weeping openly. "Oh, Mrs Stannard, she had such a terrible life and then this…you see, I know who she is. She's Sal, I know she is."

She said the same to the police constable who interviewed her in Mr Gidley's office later on, but after ascertaining that she had seen Sal at close quarters on one occasion only, and peered at a child resembling her in a backyard, and then from an upstairs attic window which gave no clear view, he seemed disinclined to believe her. "We shall make enquiries. There has been no report of a missing child."

There wouldn't be. Nobody cares about her. Had she spoken aloud? Probably not.

The young police constable made notes, licking the end of his lead pencil constantly whilst he appeared to ponder on what he was writing down in a grubby notebook.

"You will let me know the results of your investigations, won't you?"

"Don't know about that, miss. It would be irregular. You'll hear if anyone is apprehended for the foul deed. It will be reported in the press."

"You will enquire at the house in Blackfriar's Lane, won't you?"

"All that can be done will be done, miss."

Hannah had to content herself with that but as she told Mrs Stannard she had little confidence in anyone ever being brought to justice. "I am not at all sure that if a police constable actually witnessed a murder, he would be able to describe the killer. I don't think that man could read or write properly. But I am sure the child now in the mortuary is Sal."

Mrs Stannard thought she should take time to recover from the shock and return home, but Hannah was adamant that the best plan was to occupy her mind and walked to the classroom.

What a difference! Bleak walls were now covered with pictures, charts and maps and the place, almost, if not quite, transformed. The little girls, however, were subdued, bent over their slates.

The influence of Miss Phipps, Hannah decided, and trying to banish harrowing thoughts and images from her mind, she informed her pupils that they were to learn the first two verses of the Christmas song or carol called *The Holly and the Ivy.*

"I shall sing it and you will learn and follow my lead." Her pupils looked doubtful and with good reason because no sooner were voices raised in song than the door burst open and Miss Phipps, clad in unrelieved black, stalked across the room.

"We cannot hear ourselves think, Miss Morley. Such a cacophony of screeching. This is not teaching. It is…it is utter rubbish! Where does holly and ivy feature in the Nativity story? I don't recall the *running of the deer* in the streets of Bethlehem. So what explanation have you?"

"It is traditional," was all Hannah managed. "A cheerful tune and relatively easy words. I thought…"

"My advice is that you stop thinking. It obviously causes trouble. You have the brains of a gnat."

Hannah began to shake; no doubt partly a reaction to the morning's events, but anger threatened to engulf her.

"May we step outside, Miss Phipps. There is something I wish to say."

"Well, I do not wish to hear it." She turned to leave the room but Hannah was at the door first.

"Miss Phipps, today I watched a child die, her throat had been cut and she had been left for dead on waste ground," she hissed. "Her life had held no colour or affection, nothing good or to be remembered for the right reasons. My pupils have had miserable existences and I am determined to make their lives better…and may I be damned if I don't."

Miss Phipps took a step back into the room and appalled at her own temerity Hannah put a hand over her mouth. She had crossed a line and even Mrs Stannard and Mr Gidley might consider her dismissal.

"You knew the child? You recognised her?" The woman's pale blue eyes widened and held Hannah's gaze. "What did you say was her name?"

"I didn't, but it was Sal. She lived next door to my lodgings, I am sure of it. It was an appalling shock to see her lying there like a wax doll…to see her take her last breath."

Miss Phipps seemed on the point of saying something but thought better of it, but as if reconsidering she said, "Quite dreadful, if you wish to speak of it, if you need a listening ear…"

"Thank you, Miss Phipps, and I apologise for the choice of carol. Maybe the children might learn something you consider more suitable? I have seen a copy of a recently published volume, *Hymns for Little Children* and there is one entitled *Once in Royal David's City.*"

"Oh, do as you wish. You always do, anyway. I am past caring."

What a contradiction the woman was: sharp-tongued and sarcastic, harsh with the girls, but she had offered a listening ear! And Hannah had seen her running her hands through Mollie Tinsley's hair. She wondered how Mol was keeping up with Miss Phipps' class of older girls.

*****

The next day there was great excitement. With the permission of the guardians, the offer of a tall fir tree from a farmer acquaintance of Mr Gidley had been accepted. News spread like wildfire and with it news also of the beef dinner that was arranged for Christmas day.

"Plum puddin' too… Och, my girls will be busy in the kitchens," announced Agnes Blair. "It'll nae be a day off for them."

"It won't be a day off for any of us," Mrs Stannard said ruefully. "I hope you'll join us Hannah and you may leave after the meal. The men and boys will eat at noon and the women and girls an hour later. It'll be like the feeding of the five thousand. I forgot to tell you that some of the guardians and their families show their support by coming along and watching the paupers eat." Hannah raised an eyebrow and the matron concluded, "Last Christmas there was such a twitching of fine skirts and an obvious fear that the wearers might 'catch something.' It was quite horrid of me but I rather wished a flea might take a flying leap!"

"So you were here last year then. Aren't most of the staff newly appointed?"

"Mr Gidley and I arrived about the same time, just before last Christmas and my goodness, what changes a year has made. Last season saw an outbreak of influenza and the weather so cold that for weeks on end the windows were coated with ice on the inside. The basement kitchens were completely inadequate so I am thankful the new kitchen block is now built. Do you like statistics, Miss Morley?" She did not wait for a reply. "One hundred and seventy gallons of tea are brewed at a time and the racks for potatoes look as if they would hold an acre of them!"

"I am constantly astonished by the size of the place; the separate blocks, the huge exercise yards, the infirmary wards…"

"You have seen little of it yet. There are fever and itch wards, the lying-in ward, not to mention more and better accommodation for the lunatics and epileptics; nurseries and other classrooms for pupils. Under construction is housing for a schoolmaster and another schoolmistress who will live-in. It is costing a fortune, literally. Over fifty thousand pounds I have heard."

Hannah felt privileged to be part of it and said so.

"Well, the next part is to decorate the fir tree that is being delivered one week before Christmas. Mr Gidley would like the schoolchildren to make decorations and hang them from the branches. He has ordered coloured paper for the making of cornucopias and yet another of his chapel friends is donating barley twists and sweetmeats. He is like an excited child himself and insists that he is doing the rounds of the classrooms making the deliveries in person."

Next day his entrance caused a stir and a ripple of anticipation went around the room. As the Master burst in carrying a pile of boxes, followed by two elderly women inmates who were equally laden, she was reminded of Mr Fezziwig, a favourite character in Mr Dickens's *A Christmas Carol.* He positively oozed goodwill and seemed delighted with his own version of it.

"Miss Morley, good morning to you, and to all of you too," he greeted the girls." Come along…" he went on pleasantly to his two assistants, "Put the boxes on Miss Morley's desk. You may leave us now, thank you." Having deposited his own pile of boxes which seemed about to fall to the floor, he turned to survey the room. "Splendid, absolutely splendid. What do you say, you girls?"

Only Fran Noone stood up. "It's grand, sir. Thank you very much, sir."

"Which picture do you like best? Come on, you tell me, lass." He addressed a child who bit her lips and hung her head. "Well, I shall tell you which is *my* favourite. It is Jesus blessing the children. Look at the blue sky and the sunshine and all those happy faces. What about you, Miss Morley? Which do you like best?"

He had the attention of every girl in the room and they seemed to hang on his words and wait eagerly for her reply. She matched his mood.

"I love the Nativity scene. The baby and the shepherds, the shining star, and best of all the old donkey!"

"Quite, quite, and I have another bit of excitement." He turned to Hannah. "Surprises are fun but it is good to anticipate treats, wouldn't you say? I have invited a band to play for us. You know, trumpets and flutes and a big bass drum." He proceeded to march around the room pretending to blow a trumpet and eyes widened further. They stretched even more when Miss Phipps opened the door with such violence that it flew back and hit the wall. She came to a halt, staring at the master as if he was a drunk on Bridge Street.

"Miss Phipps, my good lady! You mustn't feel left out. We shall be bringing in materials for *your* pupils. I shall expect masterpieces, no less, but the main thing is to enjoy the season and its preparations." She looked at him as if he had taken leave of his senses. "Come along, Miss Phipps, I wish to make the acquaintance of the older girls."

*****

It seemed that Sal's body was to be buried with undue haste as if, thought Hannah, she was to be tidied away before seasonal celebrations began. The police had completed their enquiries and come up with the obvious statement that she had died at the hands of a person or persons unknown. Yes, they had acted upon Hannah's statement but on visiting the address nobody knew anything about a missing child. Hannah was told this by Mr Gidley.

"But my mother and I saw the child in the backyard next door," she protested.

"A visiting child. No children live in the house, or so they were informed."

"Then they were misinformed, I am sure of it. What about Sal's funeral?"

Mr Gidley shook his head sadly. "It will not be a pauper's burial and she will not go un-mourned. There will be at least six of us in attendance and the Reverend James Christie is to inter her in the parish churchyard and not the pauper's graveyard here. I think it will be appropriate to place a wreath on her little grave…" he mused to himself and seemed lost in contemplation.

Hannah suspected that he had leaned heavily on the guardians to obtain permission for a light oak coffin to be made, quite beautiful, the wood gleaming and brass handles adorning the sides. Either that or he had the financial support of chapel friends and some of them, she decided, swelled the band of mourners who stood beside the newly dug grave in the churchyard. Representing the workhouse and apart from herself were the Master and Mrs Stannard, Agnes Blair, who wept noisily, Dr Lisle and two other men whom she assumed were guardians.

The Reverend Christie, visibly moved, dispensed with some of the Anglican burial service and spoke of the brevity and uncertainty of life, of mysteries beyond our comprehension and likened the unfortunate child to a fallen sparrow, noticed by God and now safe and at peace in the hollow of His hand. "We are

78

unsure of this little one's name but let us call her Sally, for everyone must have a name." He glanced at Hannah who was wiping her eyes on a lace trimmed linen handkerchief.

Returning his glance, she stiffened as she noticed behind him and at least fifty yards away on the other side of the churchyard a cloaked and motionless female figure standing beside and almost merging with a tall ancient yew tree.

Was she an apparition? A spectre come to watch the sombre and sad proceedings? Or, and this was more alarming, someone who knew more about the circumstances and death of this tragic girl than was known to those present. On a day when wisps of fog shifted and mingled with the breath of mourners in the still cold air, there was a sinister air about the hooded figure and Hannah shivered.

She turned towards Mrs Stannard who was at her side, hoping she would follow her gaze, but even as she did so the figure disappeared as if aware of Hannah's intent.

Later she mentioned the incident to the matron but she was almost dismissive. "I am afraid many people have a morbid interest in death and news will have filtered through that this child had been the subject of a police investigation. Some sad person with not enough to fill their days, no doubt." She sighed heavily and pushed back strands of her mousey coloured hair.

"Now Hannah, I was wondering whether your mother might wish to join us on Christmas day. As far as she is concerned, it will be very civilised. Mr Gidley has relations coming from Yorkshire who will stay. There are rooms for them in one of the new blocks, but rather than be alone for a good part of the day Mrs Morley may wish to accompany you and should that be so we will provide transport."

How thoughtful! How kind! Hannah was taken aback although recognising that the last place her mother would wish to be on Christmas day was in the workhouse, albeit as a privileged visitor.

"My dear, you don't have to concern yourself over me," her mother greeted her that evening and waved a piece of paper in her direction. "I have heard from Mrs Mariah Simpson who suggests that I spend a few days with her over the festive season. No doubt she guesses that you will be occupied for much of the time but stresses that she herself would welcome my company.

Truth to tell, I would like to warm myself at her log fire and hear the village gossip and see old acquaintances. Besides, I would dearly like to attend a Christmas day service in Longwell Church."

"Then you shall, Mama. But how are we to get you there? I am not sure that we can afford a cab and you can hardly sit on the back of a carrier's cart!"

"Mariah Simpson has thought of that too. The Reverend Horatio Lovatt-Browne has a cousin, a lady I gather who is to spend the season with him, and she will be passing this way. Of course I cannot have her coming here, it is too dreadful, but something can be arranged..." she ended vaguely.

"Then you must write and accept, and we will prepare some kind of wardrobe for you and make plans. It is a splendid invitation...oh, and we must buy a suitable gift for Mrs Simpson. I came across a shop selling delicious looking bon-bons and the most exquisite artificial flower arrangements and table decorations that would brighten any home."

"You don't mind, my dear, do you? It means you will be free to spend more time at your work and I know you love to be with *your* little girls...and you tell me they have a tall decorated tree and there is to be a brass band..."

Did she mind? Just a little bit, Hannah thought. Privately she had planned a few treats and surprises for her mother and they had been going to decorate their own small tree in the attic room as a surprise for Rosa. Well, she could go ahead with that and she must not spoil Belle's happy anticipation because her mother deserved a few pleasures and interests which had been sadly lacking for many months.

"Truly, I am delighted for you. If you don't wish the Reverend's cousin to come here, and I fully understand, perhaps you might be collected at the apothecary's. I am sure they would permit you to sit inside for a while or so."

"You are so clever, dear," murmured Belle. "I don't know what I would do without you. You are your father's child in every way. You nursed me through that horrid bronchial trouble and..." she broke off and called Hannah to the window. "Oh, dear me, and it is such a miserably cold day for anyone to be outside." Hannah's heart beat fast. Surely she had not made a mistake over the mortally injured child taken to the workhouse? Surely it couldn't be Sal outside in the freezing air.

****

Chapter Eleven

The pair of them gazed down into the backyard next door where a young woman leaned against the wall of the house, her body slumped in an attitude of despair and weariness. Dark hair fell to her shoulders and she wrung her hands; whether to warm them or as testimony to her obvious distress, Hannah could not be sure.

As they watched the woman…no, she was little more than a girl…turned her head as if listening, then straightened herself and stood erect, pulling a mantle around her, but not before Belle and Hannah had noticed her bulging abdomen. As Belle tried to pull Hannah away, the girl glanced up and must have seen the pale blobs of their faces at the window. Even from a distance her expression was one of entreaty.

"Poor girl, she looks miserable, all alone and having a baby," whispered Hannah.

"Do you know what I think, Hannah?" her mother spoke slowly. "It could be that girls, unmarried that is, and in a certain condition, come next door to have their babies." An air of suppressed excitement shook her, as thoughts tumbled over one another. "It would explain the cries from the attic room through the wall. I should have known. God knows I could not suppress my cries when you were being born. One should not speak of such things but you are a doctor's daughter and you have heard talk."

"Mama, there is something I have not told you. Do you remember that soon after we arrived some weeks ago, I told you about the poor child I had met in the street outside? A small girl that horrible rough woman called Sal? Well, Sal had only that minute told me that someone named Polly had killed a little baby."

"Oh, Hannah!" Belle put a hand over her heart. "You don't think…no, such things don't happen. But suppose, just suppose that girls do give birth next door…well, many a baby dies at birth. I expect one did and Sal saw something. It would account for what she said. A child distraught by the sight of a dead infant, being wrapped or carried, a mother's cries and so on."

Hannah considered whether to tell her mother about the child brought to the workhouse, injured and dying, whom she was sure was Sal. So far she had not mentioned it or the funeral. No, she would say nothing to distress Belle although she was privately certain that she was sturdier in mind and body than was the impression given by a succession of minor ailments and her complaints. Besides, she did not frame the thought but it hovered in the back of her mind; Sal had seen or thought she had seen something and Sal was dead.

Now she recalled other curious incidents; there were indeed cries from beyond the wall, and when she had gone next door with the tartan dress, the podgy moon-faced woman had been expecting someone and it had almost certainly not been a friend as she declared. Hannah's thoughts returned to the occasion and she recalled the sharp, accusing tone. "Oh! And what about the foggy night when someone had been bundled into a coach..." She shuddered.

"Mama," she said, changing the subject, "you must certainly accept Mariah Simpson's invitation. It will do you good to get away. I shall be perfectly all right and will try to make sure Rosa has some good moments."

"You mean Leary. I suppose *she* could always accompany you to *that place* for their celebrations."

"I am not in need of company," Hannah replied firmly. *And Rosa would be about as keen to enter the workhouse as you yourself,* she thought. "But I shall keep an eye on her in your absence."

*****

"Molly Tinsley's gone, miss," Fran Noone greeted her next morning when having helped wash and dress the smaller children Hannah supervised those she regarded as *her* girls.

"Gone where? Is she ill?"

"Don't know, miss. I think she went last night. She had supper but wasn't there for bed." That was Fran, echoed by another child who added that she was quite sure Molly had not been ill or sickening for anything. "She ate all her bread and bacon. It was fatty, miss, but she ate it. See what I mean?"

Hannah was determined to ask Miss Phipps for information and came straight to the point when the women met at the end of lessons. The odour of stale sweat was once more evident. Why didn't the woman wipe her under-arms with a slice of fresh lemon which would counteract odours?

"Molly is a lucky girl, Miss Morley, although it is no business of yours. She was picked to undergo domestic training at an establishment in the country. She will be able to get a better job than scullery maid or maid of all work. It is a step up for her."

"But she is only nine, possibly ten. Surely she'd be better learning to read and write properly?"

"You think you know it all, don't you, Miss Morley? Well, you don't. What does your sort know about anything? You are an ignorant young woman and that is my last word."

"It is not mine, Miss Phipps. Why couldn't Molly have said goodbye to her friends? Why should she be whisked away just before Christmas? She would have loved the band and singing."

"Who is to say she won't have the same where she is now?" Miss Phipps replied, quite forgetting that she was supposed to have spoken her last word on the subject. "Besides, most of the celebrations are pagan nonsense." With that, she turned her back rudely and walked off.

Later Hannah had the temerity to knock on the Master's door. "Come along in," she was invited and opened the door cautiously. "Sit down, lass, what's the trouble?" It wasn't her business, that was true, but she *had* to know more about Molly Tinsley's whereabouts. Would it be possible to visit the motherless girl?

"You do well to concern yourself," John Gidley said when he heard the reason for her visit, "but rest assured nothing is amiss. One of our guardians is acquainted with a philanthropist, a wealthy man who is eager to help those who can't help themselves. It had to come to his attention – don't ask me how – that young untrained servants were often put upon and bullied. Worse, there are cases where girls have been starved, beaten and even worked to death." He sighed unhappily and placed his podgy hands together on the desk. "This man's intention is to have them receive basic training and place them with good families, maybe a shopkeeper's or even a vicar's, where they should be well treated. I doubt they'll be valued much for that's not the way of the world, but let's hope they are respected. What do you say, Miss Morley?"

"It is a worthy idea but why did Molly leave so suddenly?"

"That is easily explained. We had a guardian's meeting last night, discussing Christmas plans and so on, and Mr Jasper Meredith…you've met him…told us that his friend had a place for another suitable young girl, but that others were interested and we should make a quick decision. The long and short of it is Miss Phipps, when requested, suggested the child Molly Tinsley. The relieving officer will check on her progress, be assured."

"Will she be permitted visitors, sir? How far away is this…establishment?"

"Twelve miles, out towards Bolton way, called Brookwood, I think he said. No visitors to begin with, I'm told, as it is unsettling. Frankly, I think a friendly face is a comfort but it's not for me to say in this instance. Is that all, Miss Morley?"

She jumped to her feet murmuring an apology for taking up his time. "I like to keep a finger on the pulse, so to speak," he told her, "and I like my staff to take an interest in their charges, so save your apologies, lass, and help us get ready for the Christmas season. The young children are to receive gifts, courtesy of local traders and shopkeepers. Spinning tops and balls, picture books and the like. The carter is out collecting them." He rubbed his hands together. "Have your pupils finished making decorations?" She nodded. "Good, good, the tree will look splendid."

*****

Sam Webster grinned from ear to ear when Hannah entered the apothecary shop and as usual, he flicked back the fair fringe that threatened his eyesight. Yes, he was sure that 'old man Lawson' would not object to Mrs Morley waiting in the premises for her conveyance. Would Hannah be waiting with her, he asked hopefully.

She smiled and raised an eyebrow. "The season of goodwill being upon us and all that, I've permission to leave early and see

Mama on her way, and I shall arrange for a hansom to transport us here from Blackfriar's Lane."

Sam, it seemed, had only Christmas day as a holiday and was spending it with his widowed father and older sister who kept house for them. "You'd like Eliza, she's nice," he said simply.

The next two days saw a flurry of activity as Belle fussed over clothes to be packed in a large highly patterned carpetbag. Rosa, when she appeared, eyed the preparations with dismay but Hannah reassured her that *she* was not going away and planned to obtain a small potted tree that they might decorate together. The girl appeared very anxious and Hannah wondered whether the male caller and his unwelcome attentions were on her mind. It wouldn't do to ask because if it wasn't the case, she would merely arouse alarm.

"If Mrs Wilson agrees you can come with me to the workhouse," she offered. "There's to be a brass band and treats."

"I'm never goin' back there." Rosa's lips tightened. "Bad things happen there."

"It's getting better, lots of improvements. I wouldn't lie to you and I tell you truthfully that the new master and matron are trying to make life more pleasant for everybody. We have a big tree covered with decorations the children have made from coloured paper and scarlet cord. At the very top is a big silver star. No candles, though, because the tree might catch fire. The candles are on the sills and in wall sconces and we are putting up streamers."

"I don't care. I'm not going."

"Then I shall see you on my return and if possible, we shall be cosy together. I expect you are making Mrs Wilson's Christmas dinner?"

"She's going out," Rosa said, "She's always out and good riddance. But I'll be all right, miss."

Which is worse? wondered Hannah. *To have Mrs Wilson breathing down your neck or to be alone on Christmas day? Well, she would make haste to return in the late afternoon and keep Rosa company.*

*****

After bidding farewell to a couple of chattering middle-aged customers, Sam dusted a chair beside the counter and invited Belle to be seated. His boss, the apothecary Mr Lawson, emerged from the back room and shook her hand.

"Welcome, dear lady. Had you a good journey?" Hannah suppressed a smile. The hansom had travelled two streets only but for her mother it had been a big excitement and her cheeks were pink, adding prettiness to her dainty features.

Whilst she and the apothecary were exchanging pleasantries, Sam button-holed Hannah, asking about her plans and expressing an interest in what he called the 'goings-on' at the workhouse.

"I wish Rosa would accompany me on Christmas day," she told him. "I don't like the child to be alone. But she adamantly refuses although she is frightened of someone who visits the house."

"My sister would welcome her. Eliza's kind and friendly. Tell you what, I'll give you our address. It's not a mile away, Chandler's Court, off King Street." He scribbled on a notepad and tore off the sheet. "There you are." He handed it to Hannah, ignoring a stern look of reproach from his employer. Then turning to Belle, he announced dramatically, "Your carriage awaits, madam!"

A neat carriage pulled by a black horse was halting outside the business premises.

"Ah, a Brougham," remarked Sam who was showing off a bit, thought Hannah. "I shall carry your bag, Mrs Morley."

Her mother embraced her warmly and mentioned that Mr Lawson was most obliging. "We have agreed that I shall send letters to you here, Hannah, as we are uneasy in our minds about …you know who," she finished in a whisper.

The coachman, not liveried but well attired and attentive, helped Belle into the carriage where she was greeted by another lady with whom she was instantly engaged in conversation. Hannah, standing on the pavement, peered inside before the coachman slammed the door and felt relief wash over her. Mama's travelling companion seemed pleasantly disposed towards her and her mother had been starved of normal company. Perhaps she had not acknowledged the depths of her mother's isolation or the strain of caring for her but in truth if this was a happy break for Belle, it also afforded *her* respite.

"Now don't forget," Sam told her, "The child is welcome and yourself also, Miss Morley, which goes without saying." He blushed furiously and brushed back his blonde hair in what she now realised was a nervous gesture.

"You are a good friend, Sam, and I am very grateful," Hannah said as the coachman, having taken his seat at the front of the carriage, shouted an instruction to the horse which moved off briskly.

****

Chapter Twelve

"Got rid of your mother, then," Mrs Wilson opened the door of number fourteen and Hannah felt annoyance rise. The woman was spiteful but she was determined not to rise to the bait.

"A stay with a friend will do her a lot of good," was her reply as she passed the woman and made for the stairs.

"And you, Miss Morley? What are your plans, may I ask? A young admirer keeps you in town, maybe?" The coldness of her landlady's eyes was chilling but her interest seemed real enough.

"I am a working woman and shall be occupied with my charges." She had never informed Mrs Wilson about her work but word got around and she probably knew. "What about yourself?" she enquired, "and what about Ro...I mean Leary?"

"I shall be absent for part of the day at least. The child will be here to admit you when you return. What time do you expect that to be? I do not give keys to lodgers." There was a sneering note in her voice and not for the first time Hannah noticed that she was well spoken so had probably fallen on hard times. That was easily done as she and Mama knew too well, but the woman's tone was aggravating and Hannah was not going to hint that her intention was to spend hours with Rosa.

"Oh, late, I expect," was her airy reply. "There will be a great deal going on."

Despite the workhouse routine, preparations were afoot. Huge bundles of holly were brought in by the carter, a sad faced, sick looking individual whose legs seemed to be giving him trouble. Inmates decorated the main hall and lofty dining room, and there were low murmurings as the job was completed. The boys, balancing on shaky ladders, hung paper decorations on the upper branches of the fir tree that had been placed in the entrance hall to the main building and later the girls hung cornucopias filled with sweets on the lower branches. Their low exited chatter reminded Hannah of birds and that in the city she saw few of them apart from quarrelsome starlings and sooty pigeons. She missed the noisy rooks and multitude of small birds that had frequented the gardens and fields of Longwell; the blackbird's liquid notes, the coo-croo of collared doves, and when darkness fell the mournful cry of a predatory owl.

"Christmas morning is no different to any other although being Sunday there will be no lessons," Mrs Stannard reminded her. "With so many people under our roof we have to maintain a routine. There will be several sittings for the main meal and some of the guardians wish to watch the children enjoy their beef. That's before they scuttle off to dine on goose and all the trimmings. I am merely making an observation, Miss Morley, not criticising." Her raised eyebrows told another story and Hannah realised how refreshing and likeable was the matron. She and Mr Gidley made a good team.

On Christmas morning, she rose as usual and making her way to the kitchen presented Rosa with a little parcel containing a hand-sewn purse fashioned from green velvet. "Oh, miss," breathed the child when she discovered half a crown lurking in its depths, "did you know it was there?"

"Well, of course, you silly muffin, I put it there and Mama made the purse. I suggest you hide it from Mrs Wilson and don't say a word. Maybe the less we tell her the better, and she does not know that I shall return earlier than usual and we shall deck our own tree. I shall be able to bring some food back with me and we shall make our own fun." She dropped a kiss on top of Rosa's unbecoming cap. "You won't be wearing this tonight. We shall brush your lovely dark hair and turn you into a beauty!"

Breakfast gruel was augmented by jam spread on freshly baked bread and whilst they were still seated in the dining room, the children were presented with the gifts donated by local shopkeepers. Two hours later they gathered around the Christmas tree in the main entrance hall to sing carols and festive songs. Mothers with babies and very young infants were seated close to the tree, Mr Gidley having ordered that chairs be brought for the purpose. Girls were ranged on one side of it and boys on the other. Adults, segregated again, lined the walls.

Hannah was wearing a green dress with ample skirts supported by hoops and fashioned with bell shaped sleeves; around her shoulders was a Paisley shawl. The dress had been new two years ago. She knew that many people knowing of her father's death only a year ago would be utterly shocked at what appeared to be a lack of respect. But Papa had been adamant in his strong dislike for "mourning crows." It had been a small joke between them because as a little child she thought he had hated the birds that cawed from the elms every morning. How they had laughed when she was old enough to understand.

"May I compliment you on your admirable taste, Miss Morley? Why! The sight of you must cheer everyone present." Dr Marcus Lisle was at her side, immaculate in a dark well-cut suit, a gold watch and chain visible.

"There is at least one person it fails to cheer," Hannah responded noticing Miss Phipps standing a few feet away, her sharp eyes taking in every detail of Hannah's attire. The woman herself was dressed in purple and it occurred to Hannah that she might be coming out of mourning which would account for the sombre colours she wore. Perhaps one should make allowances.

"Problems there, Miss Morley?" It was tempting to confide some of the difficulties but now was neither the place nor time. Besides, she knew next to nothing about the medical officer and he may be better acquainted with the unfortunate Miss Phipps than she realised.

"Nothing I cannot handle. Let us say she has her own ideas about teaching and the work we do here."

"Discreet as well as attractive." He moved a step closer and Hannah, still with the unsavoury Miss Phipps in mind, stifled the desire to laugh as she pictured herself applying lemon juice to her armpits that very morning. "Have I said something amusing?" He looked quite anxious.

"Of course not. Oh, look, Mr Williams the tailor is going to accompany the children on his violin. I heard his wife is very ill and Mr Gidley has permitted the younger daughter to stay here for a week or so whilst the poor woman recovers. The older girl runs their home."

"And I heard that the carter may be off work for a while. Badly ulcerated legs which I have examined for myself, but Mr Gidley is not recording it because the man would lose his pay should it come to the attention of the guardians."

"But *you* are one of them and you have just told *me*!"

"Ah, but I am a reformer and you are discreet. I hear the little ones are going to sing *Silent Night*; I believe the English translation was published within the past year or so."

The mellow notes of the violin rose and fell and the sweet voices of the youngest children overseen by their nursery nurse sang the first verse. Other onlookers hummed the tune until the hall buzzed with the sound.

"My girls are singing *The Holly and The Ivy* just to annoy Miss Phipps!" she added, unable to resist the temptation. Marcus Lisle let out a loud laugh and the subject of his mirth glared disapprovingly.

"You have a bad influence on me," he told her and she suppressed the inclination to tease and reply that she certainly hoped so! After all, he might mistake her meaning and in any event, Mama would say that even to imagine such a reply was bold and forward. Instead she asked if he was attending the festive meal along with other guardians. No, he was not. He felt it patronising in the extreme.

Mr Gidley was in his element, pretending he was conducting Mr Williams and encouraging the singers and audience alike. "Oh dear," remarked her companion, "someone is *not* amused. I think it highly likely her sense of humour has been surgically removed."

"I have wondered whether Miss Phipps has been bereaved," Hannah said seriously. "If so, we should be more sympathetic."

"How right you are, kind-hearted Hannah Morley. Now, I will slip away and hope I may enjoy your company on another occasion."

After the singing of half a dozen more carols, her own pupils acquitting themselves well, the inmates filed out of the hall to the accompaniment of Mr William's competent playing.

Later, in the dining hall which was decked with evergreens and where candles gleamed, Hannah's pupils tucked into roast beef, potatoes both boiled and baked, and thick gravy. She attended to them and rejoiced in the scene. She had expected more chatter but the youngsters were almost as subdued as usual and bearing in mind that Miss Phipps may have her own sorrows and concerns, she attempted to draw her into conversation. "What a festive transformation in here."

There was no reply, merely a toss of the head. Then a group of people were being led into the dining hall by Mr Gidley who appeared less than happy. Well attired men with their ladies, the women wrapped in furs and wearing the most fashionable of dresses with wide hooped skirts that swept the floor. They stood watching the children eat, occasionally standing behind one or other of them to observe more closely, as if the poor young things were specimens in a zoological garden, thought Hannah indignantly.

Mr Jasper Meredith was present, accompanied by a fair-haired woman who was almost certainly his wife and two young daughters who resembled their mother. Exquisitely dressed in flounces and a flurry of petticoats, the girls sniggered behind their hands and whispered as they pointed to one or other of the young inmates. Hannah was aghast at such a breach of good manners and wished she could slap their silly faces or pull them around the room by their crimped golden hair.

She was sure others must be thinking the same and looked across at staff members, just in time to catch an exchanged glance between Miss Phipps and Mr Meredith.

Of course, there was nothing flirtatious or improper about it, she considered, but something, some understanding had passed between them, she was sure of it. Then she remembered. Mrs Stannard saying that Mr Jasper Meredith was acquainted with Miss Phipps' one-time employers and it was he who had recommended her to the board of guardians.

"May I help you, Miss Morley?" The Reverend James Christie was at her side, his brown hair in need of a barber, his eyes merry as he offered more slices of meat to children who seemed bewildered by such plenty. "Isn't it good to see such largesse? Public subscription has paid for the feast but I hear a few of the guardians have dug deeply too."

"I hope the children are enjoying it but they are very subdued."

"That is how they are trained to be. Most will go into service or apprenticeships and will be taking orders for years if not until the end of their days. My hope is that with the New Broom, our good Mr Gidley, there may be changes, but he cannot change a whole system. Are you staying for the short service and then to hear the brass band?"

"Who is Miss Popular, then?" sneered Miss Phipps when she seated herself beside Hannah, the service just beginning. More carols, a vibrant illustration of the true meaning of Christmas when the Reverend told the assembled inmates of his visit to an orphanage where the children had movingly shared the donated items he had taken with him, and then the room was being prepared for a twelve-piece brass ensemble. Miss Phipps rose. "I fail to see what men blowing into brass has to do with Christmas. I have other things to attend to."

At the end of a splendid and very noisy recital, Hannah was free to leave and clutching a bag containing cold roast beef and plum cake which Mrs Stannard had pressed upon her she stepped outside to find icy puddles and a biting frost. For a moment she thought of Sal's lifeless body lying in the bleak churchyard and trembling, she pulled her cloak more closely around her shoulders and pulled on mittens, then set off determinedly. She could do nothing for Sal but Rosa was waiting.

The main streets were bright, the lamplighters having done their rounds. A few carriages of one sort and another conveyed occupants to private celebrations, and oil lights and candles burned in rooms that would be hidden when thick curtains were drawn, but for now Hannah glimpsed the inner life within some of the properties. When she came to the shops, the street gaslights illumined the front windows. Mr Lawson's apothecary shop was in darkness and she imagined Sam enjoying Christmas cheer at home.

It never ceased to surprise her that modest affluence should flourish so close to poverty; she had no sooner turned off the main street than most of the houses were so poorly lighted they were almost in darkness. Properties that a century ago would have housed businessmen and their families, professional people who kept several servants, were now divided or let to as many people as might be crammed into them. It was quiet at present, apart from the odd drunk, but later there would be scuffles and fights that erupted into the street. At number fourteen Hannah saw no glimmer of light through the glass-panelled front door.

Lifting the small brass knocker, she tapped, the sharp noise loud in the frigid air of the late afternoon. There was no response and although she knew it was futile, she turned the door handle.

To her enormous surprise the door opened into a hall that was dark and cold.

"Rosa…! Rosa!" She stepped inside, dropped the bag of food and leaving the door ajar called again. "Where are you?" Her voice had risen a notch or two as alarm flooded her. Was the girl within or had she fled because something or someone had frightened her? Why was the door unlocked? More light was needed. If she could light the oil wick and get the lamp burning or find the striking matches and light candles…but it was so difficult in the suffocating velvety darkness. Nervous and chilled, her fingers shook as they felt and fumbled on the table top, and then her full bell-shaped sleeve knocked the oil lamp to the floor where the glass shattered on the tiles.

"Rosa!" Now her voice was a high-pitched squeak and she listened for any answering sound within the house. Did the girl lie injured? Hannah's mind churned with possibilities, each more dreadful than the last. And then, and it was a moment of terror she would never forget causing the fine hairs on the back of her neck to stand to attention even as her scalp crawled, she heard within a few feet of where she stood, quiet breathing.

****

Chapter Thirteen

Think, she told herself, but it was impossible. The overwhelming impulse was to flee as Rosa must have done and darkness was her friend as she turned and crept towards the front door. Quickly, quietly, she slipped outside just as she heard a sound in the hall and knew she was being followed, her follower making no effort to be silent. There came the crunch of glass, sounds of the door being thrown back and then footsteps on the weedy gravel path.

Swiftly Hannah slid past the old gate, tiptoed a few steps along next door's path and pushed herself into the prickly depths of the holly hedge and held her breath. There was silence, and she knew someone waited for a sound that would alert them to her whereabouts. Scratched and torn, she remained silent and motionless.

She supposed five minutes, maybe more, elapsed before she heard what must be footsteps returning to shut the front door of number fourteen because the door closed quietly, but whether someone had entered or not she had no way of knowing. It was several more minutes before stealthy footsteps crunched across the gravel and passed the gate close to where she hid. Eventually the sound of them faded. But what if it was a ruse? What if someone crept back?

Allowing herself to breathe more naturally, Hannah waited and heard the sound of a horse-drawn vehicle as it turned into the street. She knew with inner certainly that it would halt close to where she hid and afraid of discovery, she fought her way through the hedge and entered number fourteen. There was no key in the lock but there was a bolt, she recalled, and this she shot home longing only to reach the comparative safety of the attic room.

Rosa must have fled, and she prayed the child had found a hiding place. Her breath was ragged as she climbed to the first floor and then negotiated the narrow attic stairs.

Although she was almost certain she was alone in the house, she had lighted no candles, then she pushed Belle's chair against the door and crossed to the trunk. That too could be used as a barricade and if Mrs Wilson returned and found herself unable to enter her own house, frankly she did not care.

Exhausted and torn, bleeding and panicky, she pulled at the trunk and heaved it across the floor. The iron bands that strengthened it scraped on the old floorboards and at the same time as a scream of pain echoed through thin attic walls, a shriek of terror issued from the trunk. She knew then the meaning of ice in the blood. Hers seemed to freeze. With trembling hands Hannah opened the lid.

From beneath linens and clothing, Rosa's terrified face appeared. Without a cap to control it, black hair framed features frozen with fear. Her mouth opened and closed but no audible words escaped. Gently, and wincing with the discomfort of deep scratches caused by the prickly holly, Hannah lifted the child to her feet and helped her out of the trunk. Sitting on the end of the bed she held her close, whispering soft words of comfort until Rosa calmed and began a halting explanation. "He...he came. You know, *that* man."

"But darling, why did you let him in? You should not have opened the door."

"I didn't. He got in."

"How, if the door was locked? Tell me exactly what happened."

"Someone came for Mrs Wilson. I didn't see her go but she must have done because...because soon after that she wasn't here. I made sure the front door was locked and hung the key on that hook in the hall like she said." She gave a deep sob as she began the next part of her story. "Because I was alone, I did something I shouldn't have. I took a nosey look at Mrs Wilson's sitting room, at all 'er things, and that's when I heard something...the front door being unlocked. I thought she must have another key but..." Rosa buried her face in Hannah's shoulder.

"You saw the man, is that it? Where did you see him?"

"He went ever so quietly down the hall to the kitchen. I didn't know what to do but I thought of you so I came up 'ere." She gave a shuddering sigh. "It's been hours."

Hannah's tired brain tried to assimilate the facts. Mrs Wilson had conveniently been called away. She had given the unusual instruction that the front door key be hung on a hook which meant *that man*, that abominable creature, had been able to insert a key and enter. And who would have provided the duplicate key? Mrs Wilson, of course.

"Rosa darling, listen to me. We are in great danger and have to be very clever. Don't ask me any questions, just do as I say. We have to get away and I think I know where we can go, but Mrs Wilson may return at any time or that dreadful man may send someone. The house may be watched. For a start, cover yourself with this." She snatched a black shawl from the back of Belle's chair which she now pulled away from the door and blowing out the candle pushed the child onto a tiny landing. "Quiet now, not a sound." Incongruously, a loud wail, followed by a scream, sounded through the wall.

In enveloping gloom, Hannah pulled back the front door bolt and as she did so heard the sound of a horse neighing. How much time had elapsed since she had re-entered the house? Half an hour, maybe. A carriage waited outside.

Lifting her skirt, she whispered to Rosa who disappeared beneath them. *Thank God she had worn this dress for the workhouse celebrations.*

With her heart fluttering rather than beating, she opened the door and leaving it ajar the pair shuffled awkwardly across the gravel. Yes, there was a small carriage waiting outside but not directly so, it was across next door's entrance. A man, the driver no doubt, was visible in the moonlight of this frosty evening, but he was slumped in his seat and huddled against the cold.

Somewhat reassured, Hannah crossed the street and although she longed to walk briskly, slowed, as Rosa, bent double beneath her skirts, threatened to cause them both to tumble. In the haste of their departure, she had brought no money and had only the clothes she wore, dress and cloak, both ripped and grubby.

They had reached the end of Blackfriar's Lane when, hearing a disturbance behind them, Hannah glanced back and saw in the moonlight the carriage turning neatly in the middle of the street and within minutes it would be level with them.

Somehow, they reached the lights of the main street at the same time as a small horse-drawn coach drew alongside. The driver, alert now, glanced at her but almost without halting turned onto the thoroughfare and whipped up his horse. Looking around Hannah was thankful to see a few other hurrying figures; then she noticed where gaslight merged with darkness a silhouetted male outline. Someone stared in their direction. She had heard so much about the man who terrified Rosa that the figure seemed almost familiar. They might not make it safely to Chandler's Court where Sam lived and that had been her intention.

It seemed a miracle that the apothecary's shop was lighted by an oil lamp on its counter and that the lean figure of Sam was bent over it. Banging on the glass door she pressed against it until he opened it. "Help me." She stumbled into the shop and he grabbed her arm.

"Sit down, Miss Morley. Whatever has happened? Has there been an accident?"

"Sam, let me come 'round the other side of the counter. I have someone with me and she must *not* be seen. As far as any onlooker is concerned, I entered this place alone." He looked bemused, uncomprehending, but her distress was genuine and to humour her, he stood aside and let her pass. "Now, Sam, stand beside me as if we are conversing, as if you were telling me what you are doing. Make it seem natural to anyone who might look in."

To his credit he did as she requested and whilst he told her that his father had been taken ill with a fever, stomach cramps and vomiting, and he feared he had contracted influenza for which he required medicinal powders, Rosa crept from beneath Hannah's skirts and was told to roll under counter and keep out of sight.

"I will explain, but later. I am sure we are being watched and Rosa *must* stay hidden whilst I leave the premises with you. I know, darling," she bent to soothe the girl. "But my friend Sam has to return home and if I stay here, it might prove dangerous for us both. I will return, I promise."

"I shall take what's needed for Father and take you with me, Miss Morley. Then *I* shall return for your young friend," Sam said stoutly.

"Please drop the Miss Morley, Sam. I am Hannah."

He took her arm and as they hurried along, she explained their situation. "I know it seems unbelievable but I think Mrs Wilson is involved in a scheme that exploits young girls. There isn't another explanation; and then there was Sal…" She told him briefly, finishing: "Mama and I think girls…you know, unmarried girls, go next door to have their babies. I suppose the babies are farmed out. There was a woman in Longwell who took in unwanted infants. *She* was kind but my father knew of a tragic case where babies were neglected and starved to death, and the woman concerned did not report it but went on receiving money for their keep."

"Not fostered out by a union, I imagine. They're supposed to keep some sort of check. A private arrangement, maybe."

Hannah didn't know but mentioned her fear that poor murdered Sal had seen too much.

"I don't know what to say." His grip tightened on her arm. "I suppose things always seem incredible when they happen close to home. Nearly there now." They had turned off the main thoroughfare and were walking on uneven cobbles. "One floor up and I warn you our apartment isn't much, but it's warm and Eliza is welcoming."

"Your poor sister. A sick father to care for and I am about to add to her burdens, not to mention Rosa. Will you really go back for her?"

"I'd do anything for you, miss…I mean Hannah. Besides, I have to be sure the premises are secure. Be careful, now, these stairs are uneven." He unlocked a door opening off Chandler's Court and Hannah saw steps leading upwards.

"Sam dear, you took your time," came a lisping female voice as a door opened at the top of the stairs and soft light flooded out. A tall slender figure stood there and as they drew nearer, Hannah saw fair hair caught into a topknot and gentle features disfigured by an ill-mended harelip. "Have you the powders? Father is worse…oh, you've brought a visitor."

No wonder the poor woman sounded dismayed. Hannah held out a hand. "I am *so* sorry, Miss Webster. I am in desperate straits and your brother is a saviour. He will explain."

To Eliza's credit she took the proffered hand and led the way into a cramped area off which led four narrow doors; one concealing steps leading to an enclosed backyard and two opening into what must be bedrooms. The fourth was open to reveal a kitchen range glowing with heat. Taking a package from her brother, she ushered Hannah into the warmth and disappeared into one of the other rooms.

"Come in, Hannah. I shall go now for the little girl. My sister will make you a cup of tea or perhaps if I show you where things are…"

He did so and took his leave, and Hannah was soon seated in blissful comfort sipping hot tea. How kind these people were especially when they had their own troubles. She gazed around the room which was homely but orderly, a scrubbed table in the middle and a sofa piled with embroidered cushions pushed against a wall. A garland of evergreens and a few jugs containing holly as well as small ornaments adorned the wooden shelf above the range and a large rug lay in front of it.

"Father has settled, for the moment anyway." Eliza entered and busied herself at the stove. "I shall ask you no questions until you have eaten. There is beef broth and fresh bread and cheese, but first I will show you my room and bring you warm water and a towel."

Hannah drained her cup and followed Eliza into a small room made comfortable with rose patterned wallpaper and a pegged rag rug beside a narrow bed that was covered with a pink and white patchwork quilt. A washstand on which was a white china bowl and matching jug stood against one wall, a split cane chair was tucked into a corner and a row of hooks had been screwed behind the door.

Soon Eliza was back with an enamel jug full of steaming water and over her arm a white towel. She made no comment but gave Hannah a lopsided smile and placed the jug on the washstand. "Cold water is in this one." She indicated the china jug and departed.

When Hannah was again seated beside the range, tucking into savoury broth and enjoying pieces of thick brown bread spread with butter, Sam returned with Rosa who was pale as tallow wax, dishevelled and on the verge of tears. He and Eliza exchanged glances. "I'll sit with Father," he offered and left the women and girl alone.

Half an hour later when they had eaten, Eliza pulled a high-backed wooden chair to the range and seating herself said quietly, "May I know your story? Whatever it is, I assure you that you will be safe tonight. You, Hannah, may share my bed and we shall make a bed of sorts for Rosa in here." Her soft lisp was soothing and attractive in its way.

"The problem is where to begin. Rosa is a maid of all work in a house where my widowed mother and I have taken lodgings," she began, and then the words started to pour out, the strange occurrences and her fear for Rosa.

Eventually Sam joined them. "Father's asleep but his breathing's rough and shallow. At least he hasn't vomited again but it'll be a disturbed night." He whispered in Hannah's ear, "I don't know what to think but there *was* a man hanging around the shop." He turned to Eliza, "Have you sorted out sleeping arrangements?"

"Of course, and I have heard the harrowing tale. Rosa *must* stay here. I don't know the implications of hiding a workhouse child who was placed elsewhere, but we shall find out. What about your work, Hannah?"

She plucked at her ruined dress. "I shall have to return to Mrs Wilson's and fetch something to wear so I'll send a message that I'll arrive late for work. And, of course, I have to look for other lodgings." She sighed wearily. "But in the morning, I may be able to face things, I'll feel brighter and more brave."

"You've been very brave, no-one more so, "Sam said firmly and Eliza nodded agreement before rising to her feet. "What a strange Christmas day for all of us." She put an arm around Rosa. "You are exhausted and I suggest a wash and bed. I'll bring blankets and you will sleep on the sofa. You'll be completely safe, my dear."

Later, in Eliza's bed which the girl had insisted she share and where in borrowed nightgown she lay straight as an arrow in case she take up too much room and prove a disturbing influence, Hannah whispered her thanks again.

"It's nothing. I am pleased to help and I am concerned for Rosa. In fact, I am concerned for all vulnerable children. I help teach in one of the ragged schools so I know what I am talking about."

"You're a very special person, I can see that. No wonder Sam is so proud of you and he is, that's obvious."

"Sam's special too," Eliza's breath was warm on Hannah's neck. "We are very close and have been since our mother died years ago. I am protective of my little brother and would hate to see him hurt." Eliza sighed and turned over. "It won't be a very comfortable night and I shall have to get up to Father every so often. He and Sam share a room but I can't leave it all to him. Oh, dear, Father is coughing again."

Through the dividing wall came the sound of painful rasping and the murmur of voices. She and Rosa *must* find new lodgings as soon as possible; these kind people bore too many burdens.

Next morning, both Sam and his sister looked fatigued and drawn but announced cheerfully that their father was no worse, in fact slightly improved. Sam was full of plans.

"First a message to old Mr Lawson. I shan't mention you, Hannah. I shall tell him truthfully that my father is ill and I shall be later than usual to the shop. I'll get a message to the workhouse and then accompany you to number fourteen and beard the lion, so to speak."

Hannah tried to smile but her spirits lowered at the prospect of meeting the woman who had been less than kind to Mama and herself and almost certainly harboured evil intentions towards Rosa.

"...As for you, Rosa," Eliza placed a pan of smooth simmered oats on the table and began dolling portions into china bowls, "you will stay here with me. You will be useful, but the main reason is your safety. You needn't go outside at all because as you know there are interior steps leading to the backyard. Sam, Father is calling again, will you go this time?"

Hannah and Rosa did their best to ease Eliza's lot after Sam departed and tidied and cleaned whilst she attended to her parent. An hour or so later, Hannah gave a gasp of surprise when Sam returned, this time with Dr Marcus Lisle in tow.

Sam, not entirely at ease, led the way into the kitchen announcing that he and the doctor had met in the main entrance hall of the workhouse and on hearing something of the story, both of Sam's sick father and of Hannah's predicament, had insisted that he return to Chandler's Court and be of assistance.

"I was already acquainted with your brother, Miss Webster, as I patronise *Lawson's Apothecary Shop*," he greeted Eliza, "and I know Miss Morley," he smiled at Hannah before turning towards Rosa, "but I have not had the pleasure of meeting this young woman." Rosa blushed prettily and hung her head in embarrassment. "I suggest I attend the patient, so lead the way, Miss Webster."

"We came by cab," Sam told Hannah, "and the doctor insists he accompany you to your lodgings." He frowned. "I suppose it means I can get to work although Mr Lawson will be there by now. When I see you this evening, we can talk. Take good care, Hannah."

****

Chapter Fourteen

"Well, Miss Morley, I insist you fill the gaps in the extraordinary story Sam told me."

They were seated in a brougham and now turned out of Chandler's Court into King Street which was humming with noise and commotion. The world was getting back to work and normal activities after a day of mainly family celebration.

"It was terrifying," Hannah told him, "Entering the house, sensing someone close by in the darkness and then hiding in the holly hedge, and finding Rosa, distraught and frightened half to death, in the trunk. I very much fear Mrs Wilson arranged for a possible assault on the girl or even an abduction. Does that sound like wild imagining?"

"Not as you tell it." He laid a hand on her arm. "There are huge social evils mostly hidden under so-called respectability. In the words of a speaker at a meeting I attended: *There is exploitation at all levels, the faces of the powerless being ground under feet climbing ladders to financial success or personal pleasure.* Well put, isn't it? See, we are in Blackfriar's Lane. Let me do the talking and then help you bring down your belongings."

"I am causing you such inconvenience but I am deeply grateful to you, and to the Websters."

"They're a nice family and Mr Lawson speaks well of young Samuel. He refers to him as diligent and reliable. Still, I don't suppose for one moment Samuel is aware of it because his employer always adds that it would not do for the young man to rest on his laurels."

Blackfriar's Lane looked as depressing as usual and number fourteen and its neighbour grubbier and more run-down than ever. As if catching her thought, the doctor said, "Not what you were used to I'll be bound, but you'll soon be out of here forever."

If Mrs Wilson was surprised to see Hannah, she failed to show it but her surly expression was ironed out as if by magic when she saw her companion who introduced himself with some exaggeration, Hannah thought, as, "a friend of Miss Morley's come to help with the removal of her belongings."

"So you are leaving us, Miss Morley, I am sorry to hear that." *Liar*, thought Hannah and wondered how much Mrs Wilson knew or guessed of the events of the previous evening. "I was going to offer you and your dear mother one of my better rooms at no extra cost, you understand."

I understand all right. Aloud Hannah said, "Thank you but I cannot remain here. You see…" She was interrupted by Marcus Lisle.

"Miss Morley arrived here last evening and found the front door open. The house was unlit and it appeared your maid had fled. May we ask if she has returned safely? Miss Morley has been very anxious about her, especially as the night was very cold."

"Leary has left me, the ungrateful girl, but you know what maids can be like. I imagine she was lonely here. It's not much of a life for a young person without a companion, but I am not in a position to keep more staff." There was a whining note in her voice.

"We shall see you are not out of pocket," the doctor said briskly. "Now, there is no need to accompany us, Mrs Wilson. I am sure you have much to attend to in the absence of your maid and Miss Morley can lead the way to your attic rooms." Did she imagine the emphasis on the last two words, Hannah wondered. No, because the landlady looked disconcerted, even uncomfortable as she moved away from the stairs and allowed them access.

"Ye gods! Don't tell me you and your mother lived up here? The room is perishing, the place quite appalling." He crossed to the window. "Not much of a view either unless one has a taste for grim backyards. I am sorry it came to this, Miss Morley. You and your mother have suffered."

"Not as much as Sal who lived next door. You know who I mean, Dr Lisle; the child that was brought to the workhouse, her throat cut. I met her soon after we arrived here and she told me something quite shocking. I am as sure as I can be that later on

Mama and I saw her in the yard…" she broke off. "Why are you looking at me like that? What have I said?"

"Miss Morley…Hannah…Gather your things together and get out of here. Forget that you ever knew anyone named Sal." He sounded angry as he opened the lid of the trunk and then after ripping clothes off hangers began stuffing them inside the trunk. A shawl and boots were thrown in whilst Hannah emptied the contents of a drawer on top of everything else. His tone had alarmed her and as they worked in silence, she felt almost afraid of him. He seemed unapproachable and remote, and it *had* to be because of what she had said.

It was as the trunk lid was lowered that a scream tore through the air and he straightened, his expression alert as he listened. "It's from next door; Mama and I think girls go there to have their babies," Hannah informed him as another cry of anguish sent icy tremors along her spine.

"Miss Morley, whatever have you and your mother got mixed up with? You realise, don't you, that I cannot leave until I have made enquiries and perhaps helped whoever is in distress. I will instruct the cab driver to return to Chandler's Court and carry your trunk upstairs. Do as I say and I will see you at your work or call upon you later. Please Hannah…"

Back at the Websters', Eliza had settled Rosa to clean brass ornaments whilst she baked bread and the pair were cosily ensconced in the kitchen. "You look exhausted, Hannah, I shall make you a hot chocolate and you will drink it before you do another thing. Are you going to your work today?" Eliza's fair hair flopped over her forehead reminding Hannah of Sam.

"I have to. I shall look out a dress," she gestured towards the trunk that now stood in a corner of the room, "and when I am presentable, I shall walk there. How is your father? Still improving, I hope."

Eliza nodded. "I am grateful Dr Lisle examined him. My mind is easier. Sam has always said what a nice gentleman he is. I believe he is very well connected. Not that it matters, of course."

After resting for a while and Eliza having pressed a grey woollen dress of her own for her, Hannah walked to the workhouse and reported to Mrs Stannard. Briefly she explained the circumstances leaving out references to Rosa. It wasn't that she mistrusted the matron but it was too easy for news to spread and the girl's whereabouts must be kept secret.

There was a slight relaxation of the rules as it was St Stephen's Day, Boxing Day as some called it, and Hannah prepared to tell her pupils stories and teach them lively poems and songs. In the end she set them to draw pictures on their slates.

Her mind darted about and her thoughts would not be stilled. There was the problem of hiding Rosa, of finding new lodgings, and of informing her mother that they might themselves be at risk owing to all that had happened; and how, she wondered, was Dr Marcus Lisle getting on? She doubted that he would be admitted to the house next door but if he gained entry, what would he find?

She discovered later in the day when she was attending a head injury in the receiving room, a young labourer who had fallen from scaffolding in one of the yards outside.

"I will take over. One can never tell how such an injury will affect the patient." Mrs Stannard was at her side. "Blood loss does not indicate the extent of damage. We shall have to admit him…oh dear…and the receiving ward is full. Miss Morley, I have just met with Dr Lisle and he wishes to speak with you. I suggest you use the side room."

The side room was where Sal had died and Hannah clenched her fists in an effort to control her emotions as she entered. *He looks tired*, she thought as Marcus Lisle rose from a battered chair to greet her. "Sit down," he invited, "and please tell me everything you know about your ex-neighbours."

"Well, it's only a few weeks since Mama and I took lodgings with Mrs Wilson. I met Sal right at the start, but you know about her, and you know too what we believed about the girls giving birth, but I *have* been thinking about other things. Sometimes a carriage halted outside and on one very foggy night when I could see nothing, I heard sounds of someone being lifted or pushed into such a vehicle."

She halted, aware of his unwavering stare. "There was the occasion when I took a dress next door, Mama had altered it for Sal. Incidentally it was taken to a pawnbroker's. I am sure someone else was expected that night and the woman who opened the front door imagined I *was* that person and spoke harshly. Then she pretended a friend was due to arrive." A shadow crossed her features and he was quick to notice it.

"Go on," he urged. "You have thought of something else. I know it."

"I wondered whether you had gained entry and whether you came across a woman named Polly?"

"I *was* admitted. At least I barged my way in announcing that I was a doctor and I owe it to you to tell you what I discovered, but no, there was nobody named Polly as far as I can tell. There were two women who seemed to be in charge of things and they hardly spoke in my presence. The older, about fortyish, was referred to as Nellie. I can't recall the other's name if I heard it but not Polly. The place is a disgrace and yes, Miss Morley...Hannah...if I may...there *was* a young woman suffering the pangs of a difficult labour."

"Will she be all right?" It was such as naive question that Hannah blushed. How could any poor girl giving birth in those circumstances be all right? And what of her future?

"She survived and so did the child, but they are not out of danger. I have my suspicions about the place. The girl was past caring, but was introduced as a young relative, visiting when her pains began, but there's no truth in that; she is a different type, altogether superior to the rough women of whom she is afraid, I am sure of it. Of course, there is nothing illegal about offering shelter to pregnant women and helping them at the birth. It would depend on other factors: what sort of arrangements were in place, the exchange of money, the welfare of mother and child."

"Maybe the babies are farmed out. But there are other things too that are worrying. Rosa, for instance. The man who visited the house with what I am sure were bad intentions and Mrs Wilson's complicity, and none of that connected with next door."

"One thing leads to another, there are sometimes undreamt-of connections, but what causes me most anxiety is your safety and that of Rosa, as you call her. If, as Sam Webster believes, you were watched and suspected of spiriting the child away, and worse, if it is thought that you know more about Sal than you do, you are in danger. A change of lodgings may not alter that."

Hannah shuddered. "Rosa is safe at present. I shall find somewhere else for Mama and myself to live and things will get back to normal. I am sure of it, Dr Lisle."

"I certainly hope so. In the meantime, I have told the woman Nellie that with or without her permission I intend to call at the house until the ailing mother and child are on the path to recovery. Promise me you will not visit Blackfriar's Lane and if you walk alone, keep to busy well-lighted streets."

By the time Hannah left the building, the weather had changed and frost had been replaced by sleet that was whipped into her face by a strengthening wind. The prospect of Eliza's warm kitchen and hot food was comforting and she must pay the Websters. She had enough money for the next few days and if Mr Gidley kept to their arrangement, she would receive a month's wages at the end of December. She would also write to her mother informing her of a change that would be welcome. Poor Mama, how she had hated the attic room, and no wonder. It must be quite wonderful for her to be back in Longwell and enjoying comforts and pleasant companionship.

Eliza greeted her pleasantly and Rosa gave a bright smile. The child's hair had been washed and tied with a red ribbon and her clothes brushed. Others of her garments had been laundered and now aired in front of the range on which a large pot bubbled and a kettle sang. Old Mr Webster was holding his own, she was informed and, if she was good enough, Hannah might keep an eye on him when Eliza went out for an hour or two. "I am helping at the local ragged school and would hate to let the children down. I have baked bread for them." She picked up an envelope. "Sam said this was delivered to the shop." Hannah recognised her mother's handwriting. "And this," she held out another, "must have been pushed through the letter box as it has no postal stamp on it."

In the privacy of the bedroom and by the light of a small oil lamp, she read her mother's words:

"...Mrs Simpson is kindness itself. We attended a delightful service on Christmas day when the Reverend Lovatt-Browne was in his element. Such beautiful wreaths and decorated pews and the church quite beautiful. How I have missed it all, my dear. I hope the celebrations at that place brought you some cheer. I could hardly bear to think of you in that frightful attic room, so maybe the alternative was better. We, that is Mariah and I, are

visiting mutual acquaintances this afternoon. Goodbye for now my dearest daughter, your affectionate Mama."

Hannah smiled. Mama was like an excited child and just as selfish, completely caught up in the activities of the moment. Was she being too hard on her? She thought not. There was something childlike about her mother, but she was very dear all the same and Hannah missed her.

The second envelope was of poor-quality paper and the uneven script in a hand unrecognised by Hannah.

She slit open the other letter and unfolded it. At first she made no sense of the scrawled sentence, the letters were badly formed and most of her workhouse pupils might have done better. Then as she deciphered the words, her heart beat faster. It was one of those hateful anonymous notes full of underlying threat: *"...I know where you are..."*

"Hannah, you look troubled. Did you receive bad news?" Eliza was full of concern as she ladled rich stew into bowls and placed them on the table. "My goodness, but you are pale."

Rosa glanced up and Hannah forced a smile. "My mother is well and very contented. I am tired after all the alarms and excitements. Tell me, what have you been doing, Rosa?" Eliza flashed her a perceptive glance and said no more.

It transpired that the girl had been immensely useful and Eliza had even sat with her feet up for an hour whilst Rosa listened in case old Mr Webster needed attention. Later Eliza sent Rosa to check on the patient and turned to Hannah. "Something is amiss. When you sat down to eat you looked as if someone walked on your grave."

Hannah pulled the note from her pocket. "This is what was pushed through the letter box. I have to find other lodgings, and quickly. You too are in danger as long as I remain here."

"It is probably some mischief maker, someone who dislikes you and wishes to cause you alarm. Can you think of anyone in particular? Have you crossed anyone?"

"Don't you see, it *has* to be connected with Mrs Wilson or Next-Door-Nellie...of course, you don't know about her; I'll tell you what Dr Lisle told me, but some other time," she finished as Rosa re-entered, flushed with the importance of being promoted from a maid of all work to nursing assistant.

Having been introduced to Mr Webster who was nothing but a mound beneath a heap of blankets, and having reassured Eliza that all would be well in her absence, Hannah watched the older girl leave, weighed down with baskets. "It's no use offering to help me," she said. "You must stay with Father, and Rosa must not set foot out of doors until we are sure she will be safe. It's a dreadful night but I have eighty or more boys waiting for me, poor young things. Keep the meal hot for Sam, he'll be home before me," she added.

Apart from tending to the old man when he coughed and holding a cup to his lips, Hannah was free to sit with Rosa beside the fire, whiling away time with storytelling. "What's your story, Rosa?" Hannah asked gently. "Do you remember anything before the workhouse?"

"I might have been born there. My mother died but I don't know when. I don't think I knew her."

"I think you may be older than you believe. I know some girls grow up more quickly than others, but you are more than nine or ten, Rosa."

"You could look it up, Miss…Hannah, I mean. They write down everything in the work'ouse."

Why hadn't she thought of it? Of course, the records of admissions and minutes of every meeting ought to be kept and those for previous years should be in Mr Gidley's office.

"I will ask tomorrow," Hannah promised. "You are a bright girl. Fancy that, I never gave it a thought."

There came the sound of the stamping of boots and Sam was home, his fair hair wet with sleet, his face tired and anxious, but his smile enveloped them both. "If Eliza's out, it means Father is improved." He rubbed his hands to warm them. "I'll go in to see the poor soul."

When he returned to the kitchen, a bowl of Eliza's thick stew steamed in readiness, bread and butter "to fill the corners" as Hannah told him, and to finish a creamy milk pudding. He sighed with pure contentment and ate heartily. When he could eat no more, Hannah took away the dishes and as Rosa jumped up to attend to the invalid, she laid the worrying note before him.

"I don't wish to cause you more anxiety but I think you should know that Eliza found this pushed through the letter box.

She thinks, or says she does, that it is fairly harmless. Someone bearing me a grudge because I have upset them in some way."

Sam examined the badly scrawled words. "I don't like it," he said. "You'd an idea you'd been followed and I saw a man loitering outside the apothecary shop, and there is no doubt the danger at number fourteen is real enough." He rose abruptly. "What if Eliza is accosted and threatened until she confesses that she knows your whereabouts? I must go and meet her."

Guilt flooded Hannah. It was she who had put the Websters in danger. In an agony of mind, she tidied the kitchen and attended to Mr Webster, still coughing but less feverish. Patiently she spooned gravy into his mouth and in answer to the unspoken question in his eyes, told him that she was a friend of his daughter and Sam had gone to meet his sister. *Please, let them come home soon. Don't let anything terrible happen to Eliza.*

It was with heartfelt relief that Hannah greeted the brother and sister when they appeared. "Almost blown home by the wind," announced Sam before he went to see his father. "It's wild out there and the sleet will turn to snow, I am sure of it."

Eliza hung her cloak beside the range and lifted the boiling kettle. "Things went well tonight. The boys are such poor young creatures, half-starved and filthy, their skin scabby and itching. We gave them soup and potatoes, and they tore at the bread. There's an astonishing woman who teaches at an industrial school during the day and an elderly man connected with one of the Methodist churches. Sometimes a charming curate calls in to lend a hand. Oh, and we had a newcomer this evening. Quite the gentleman!"

"How are you funded?"

"In our case by charitable donations and we meet in a warehouse lent by a business friend of the Methodist. You probably know the Ragged Schools Union was started in London some years ago, making it more official, but there is so much more that could be done, educationally and socially." She sipped tea and Rosa put in, "Have you ever heard people say their tea is *so* strong a mouse might tap dance on it? Hannah heard the expression somewhere. It makes me laugh."

Eliza smiled lopsidedly and put an arm around Rosa before continuing, "What worries me most is the biting cold and the lack of footwear. We have been donated blankets and clothes, so the worst rags, and believe me that's what they are, can be discarded. If only we might interest the wealthy class in the city."

"Perhaps your new volunteer?" suggested Hannah. "Is he a businessman?"

"A journalist, I think he said. Duncan something or other. There is never time to talk much but he helped organise things and talked to the boys, and he was a source of much interest, probably because he wore a watch and chain. It's a wonder he still possessed it at the end of the session!"

Sam clattered in. "Father really does seem to be mending but it'll be a while before he is up and about. Hannah…" he shifted uncomfortably, "I've been thinking about suitable lodgings for you. I mean, you are welcome to stay but there will be your mother and…"

Hannah rescued him. "I've been thinking too. Bearing in mind all that has happened, I may have conceived a clever plan, although the success of it depends on other people." She had the attention of all three and placed a hand on Rosa's thin arm. "Suppose Rosa stayed with you for a while, just until matters settle. Is that possible?"

Eliza glanced warmly at the girl. "Of course. You'd be safe here and I like your company." *She is the kindest creature* ran Hannah's thoughts before continuing. "My mother is staying in our home village and her hostess, Mrs Mariah Simpson, could almost certainly be prevailed upon to extend the stay. I propose to visit within a day or so and ask her. As for myself, I am also going to ask Mr Gidley if I may stay in the workhouse for a while. There shouldn't be any difficulty. Many of the staff have rooms there and his Christmas visitors will be departing anyway."

Sam's relief was almost palpable and then as if aware of it he hastened to reassure Hannah that his concerns were for herself and Eliza should she have been followed to Chandler's Court.

"I know it," Hannah said swiftly, putting him at ease. "And who knows, by this time tomorrow I may be installed at the workhouse!"

****

Chapter Fifteen

The weather worsened overnight and by morning snow lay several inches thick. Hannah pitied the poorly clad crossing sweepers, young boys, many of whom might have been better off under the workhouse roof. Removing a mitten, she felt in her reticule for a few coins which she pressed upon a particularly ill-nourished lad before walking slowly and carefully to her destination. Horses pulling a variety of carts and conveyances took their time despite the oaths and urgings of the drivers.

Mr Gidley greeted her with his usual bonhomie and entreated her to warm herself at his office fire. Soon she was telling him of her predicament, leaving out salient points as she had done when speaking to Mrs Stannard, and finishing with an enquiry about accommodation and the financial implications.

"Don't worry yourself about that, lass. As I see it, the only problem is the weather; it's put paid to travelling far and that means my visitors and the Welshman's daughter are stuck here for a few more days. Mrs Stannard is the one to ask and I'll see to it."

"There's something else, Mr Gidley." She told him briefly about Rosa and her promise to seek more information about the girl's origins. "Have you records of ten, possibly twelve years ago?"

"Somewhere hereabouts." He looked helplessly round the room. "You can have no idea of the chaos we inherited and we're at the point of getting past paperwork into some kind of order. Still, it should be in a leather-bound volume and I'll do my best. You say her surname is Leary?"

"That's what she is called and says she has known no other name, although she has chosen to be known as Rosa."

"Very fancy and a sight better than Leary for a lass, and I guess you had a hand in that, Miss Morley. You've a soft heart and it does you credit."

His kind tone almost persuaded her to tell him about Rosa's recent ordeal and her own involvement, but he was getting to his feet and she did the same.

Miss Phipps seemed to be sickening for something and by the sound of her cough, it might well be influenza. Had she liked the woman better Hannah would have felt more sympathy but her complaint brought out the worst aspects of her personality, and the wails and cries from some of her pupils indicated that physical punishment was being inflicted. Hannah was about to investigate, although reminding herself that it was not her business and Miss Phipps might seek retribution, when a girl burst into the classroom announcing, "Miss Phipps feels faint, Miss."

When summoned, Mrs Stannard took over, and Miss Phipps, having been revived with strong smelling salts, was escorted to her room and bed.

"I am afraid you will have two large classes to oversee, Miss Morley, and by the looks of it for the next few days. I shall not expect you in the receiving ward as you will be fully occupied but I can send a couple of the older female inmates to lend a hand."

"If I need help, I promise to let you know. I shall set work and we shall learn songs and poetry, and as the girls cannot go outside, perhaps they may do physical exercises in their classrooms?"

"Whatever you think best. Oh, and about accommodation here. It will be perfectly feasible in a week or so, but I gather you need something immediately. In that case, it will mean sharing with the Williams girl if she and her father, our new tailor, have no objections. Such a pretty girl," she added inconsequentially.

The day passed much as Hannah had planned and the pupils were very well behaved. Unnaturally so in Miss Phipps's class and several were very subdued, red smarting knuckles telling their own story. It was impossible to crowd everyone into one room so her time was spent between the classes. Whilst some copied from the blackboard onto their slates, the others learnt verses, and so it was, turn about. Walking amongst the girls in Miss Phipp's class, she cast her eye over their work and it was when she came to one particular girl, a pale weepy-eyed wisp, that she halted. The child's writing looked rather familiar. How puzzling; she had not previously seen the work of these older girls but surely…No, it was impossible that this child had anything to do with an anonymous note.

Late in the afternoon, Mrs Stannard informed her that she might make arrangements to have her belongings delivered as no objections had been made about sharing a room with Sairin Williams. "From tomorrow, which gives you time to bring your belongings." Then she added," Mr Gidley would like a word with you but nothing to worry about."

His office seemed overheated after the chill of the classrooms and the Master himself looked uncomfortably hot. The wide desk was piled with books and ledgers, and he pulled forward an impressive outsized volume, handwritten pages bound between leather covers.

"This contains some of the patchy records for the last decade or so; let me see, 1848 onwards. Lists of admissions, births, deaths and so on, but not all recorded, I am sure of it. I've glanced, no more than that, and I can see no one by the name of Leary. You are welcome to search for yourself. Of course the book remains in this room, lass."

"Thank you, Mr Gidley." She flashed him a grateful smile. "I would love to look, but tomorrow, maybe, when I am staying under this roof. I have to get back to my friends and it's been snowing all day. It'll take a while." He nodded amiably.

"Quite so, quite so. Tomorrow it shall be."

The snow muffled sounds but the pavements were well trodden. There were still a fair number of folk about and noisy sounds and harsh laughter from a couple of public houses, light from the premises spilling into the darkness which was reassuring.

There were fewer horse-drawn vehicles owing to the road conditions, but one had kept pace with Hannah for some while as she walked as quickly as she could on the freshly falling snow and then left the main street and its lights, and turned into the lane leading to Chandler's Court.

The small carriage turned too and Hannah halted, aware of incipient danger. The carriage stopped too. A moment later she attempted to run, but her boots gained no grip and she was about to fall on her face when a pair of strong arms pulled her roughly towards the vehicle.

Her screams brought no response, her wriggling body was captive and held fast. A second man, presumably the driver, came to the aid of her captor and she was bundled into the carriage followed by her aggressor.

"Shut up, I tell you. On your way, driver," and he pulled down the blinds so that the interior was black. The horse, stumbling and sliding as its hooves sought purchase, set off slowly, the small conveyance jerking and unsteady so that Hannah was thrown against the man who sat beside her and inhaled the strong smell of an expensive cologne.

"Why?" she asked croakily, fear making her faint, "Why are you doing this and where are we going?"

"Don't play the innocent. You know why. The girl, Leary, where is she? And think before you lie to me. Remember Sal. She knew too much too."

Poor little Sal lay in the freezing churchyard, but Rosa sat in a warm kitchen and was experiencing kindness at last. It should not be taken from her.

"I...I don't know." He lashed out, hitting her across the face and knocking her temple, so that her head felt as if it might snap off when she was jerked back. She flailed, her fingers catching in what felt like a watch chain. He grabbed her hand and thrust it from him angrily.

"You know damned well what I am talking about. Somehow that child got away and I warn you, lie to me and you'll fare very badly."

Although shaking with fright and her thoughts jumbled, Hannah knew that an outright lie would be foolish. Whoever this man was, he knew too much about her: of her involvement and her connection with Sam for a start. Someone must have watched the apothecary shop, and as a result of it she or Sam had been followed. Maybe Rosa had been seen with him. Tonight this man had come after her, possibly trailing her from the workhouse. An outright lie would be foolish and useless.

"I know where she *was* but not where she is now. She was going to friends in the country."

"She has no friends." There was a slight hesitation. "Where in the country?" Hannah heard the doubt creep into his cultured voice, educated and clipped.

"Someone…I don't know their names." She was inarticulate, unsure of what to say in case her words became a net that trapped her in an inescapable mesh.

"Where?" he whispered angrily against her ear and she cursed herself for a reply that might spell more trouble.

"Longwell." The word popped out of her mouth, it being the only place she knew well and one that was often in mind.

"I hope for your sake you are speaking the truth but you realise I cannot let you go, not yet anyway, Hannah Morley."

He knew her name. Well, of course, but it seemed a further intrusion into her life, a breach of privacy. How much more was known? How stupid to have mentioned Longwell. Was her mother in danger now? Would the nightmarish chain of events never end?

It was impossible to see the face of the man at her side but she did not recognise his voice and was certain that he was unknown to her. She raised a hand and stroked her painful face. At the same moment the carriage rocked to standstill and her captor made a small movement before binding a cloth over her eyes. "Where am I?"

"I am hardly likely to inform you or there'd be no need for a blindfold. Use your intelligence."

Minutes later she was handed down onto snow, a firm grip on her elbow, and the driver told to wait. Hannah strove to hear sounds other than the horse's rough breaths and a jingling harness but there were none. She calculated that they had travelled a mile or a little more, but in her fear and in darkness she had no sense of direction.

Then she was being armed across what must be pavement and through a narrow gateway, and when prickly leaves scraped her damaged face, she knew. She was being taken to the house next to number fourteen. To Next-Door-Nellie. Relief surged through her, but it was momentary because the picture of Sal's death filled her mind.

She kept silent as the door opened and she was both pushed from behind and pulled by rough hands over the threshold. A coarse voice hissed, "Right you are, sir," and she was being propelled along the hallway as the front door closed.

"Right, Miss Busybody, you'll learn to keep your nose out of what don't concern you. Up we go." She was pushed towards stairs that must be similar if not identical to those in the house next door but stumbled as her feet caught in her skirts. "Get a move on, why don't you?"

The common voice jarred and fleetingly Hannah wondered how the path of her obviously well-educated captor had crossed with that of this woman. Was she the same who had berated Sal some weeks ago? Probably, but she could not be sure.

"In here, then." A brutal shove almost sent her sprawling and then her blindfold was whipped away and Hannah surveyed her surroundings. A low iron-framed bed, a wooden chair and bare floor viewed in the light of a smoking tallow candle appeared unspeakably drab and gloomy. The intense cold made her gasp and so did the malevolence in the woman's eyes.

"We're busy in this 'ouse. You're not wanted but what was to be done with you? I 'ad no choice. I'm told to see you stay here and that's what I'll do." She turned and seconds later Hannah heard a key grating in the lock.

Almost falling onto the bed, she sat on the hard mattress and tried to still her panic. Surely, had they planned to kill her, she would have been bundled into the river. Almost certainly she was not the focus of their intentions but little black-haired Rosa, but if they discovered she had lied…what then?

Thoughts agitated. How long until she was missed? It might be days, certainly a day or two. The Websters would think she was staying at the workhouse; her mother would not expect a letter or visit while the snow lasted…only Mr Gidley might send a messenger to enquire about her absence…no, no, impossible. He did not know that she had lodged with the Websters. Dr Lisle knew but not of her current whereabouts. Mentally and physically worn, she threw herself down and curled herself into a tight ball. To her surprise, she dozed fitfully.

Whether it was the low moaning that came through the dividing wall or squeals of pain that seemed to fill the house and were to become intermittent, Hannah was unsure, but the harrowing sounds of both swelled in her aching head until it felt like bursting. Then came running footsteps and mutterings and a sense of panic about both.

The harsh voice of the woman who had admitted her accompanied the footsteps. "Nellie, we need Pol. Big trouble. We're gonna lose this one if we're not quick off the mark."

****

Chapter Sixteen

Pol? Might that be Polly? Hannah strained her ears. The desperate moaning sounds now seemed hushed but the screams and cries were as strong as ever. More footsteps and whisperings, but she could catch very little of what was being said. Something about, *"not long now,"* and *"getting rid of it."* The horror of this house and the events taking place made Hannah nauseous. Get rid of what? A body? Was someone dying? The one who moaned or the one who screeched in agony.

Just when she thought she would open her mouth and scream too, the candle flickered, spluttered and went out, the smell of rancid fat drifting around the room, and at the same time there came a thin wail, the cry of a new-born which grew lustier until it stopped abruptly. The moans had subsided into whimpers interspersed by frantic whisperings and then more running footsteps, this time along the passage outside. "Pol, we can't stop it."

Whoever Pol might be, she seemed to restore some calm, and Hannah overheard a few of her instructions, an isolated word or two here and there. *"Cloths, sheets…hot water…cold water…think…yes, before it's light."*

Her tired brain and throbbing head made her dizzy and disorientated, the absence of light adding to the sense of detachment. She wondered whether she might doze again if she lay down. Then came the sharp sound of rapping at the front door and someone cursed.

"Lord Almighty! Who the hell's that?"

Again muffled whispers followed by the loud raucous tones. "If it's that girl from Chorlton, she's started early. Put her in one of the small rooms, Nellie."

Footsteps coming upstairs, a frightened voice and then the key being turned in the lock and in the light of an oil lamp from somewhere outside the room, Hannah saw the outline of a young woman who was being hustled through the doorway. "No time now. Got a houseful. Have you started?"

There was a despairing sob and whoever had entered was left in the dark unaware of Hannah's presence whilst *she* was aware of one over-riding fact: the door had been left unlocked.

"I don't know who you are but my name's Hannah," she whispered. "I'll try and fetch help. Don't ask questions. I was locked in but will try to escape." Another sob and cautious footsteps but the girl bumped into the end of the bed and her cries grew louder. "Try not to make a noise. Are you in pain?"

"Yes, oh yes…oowh…It's the baby. It's coming." Hannah felt her heart plummet as she guided the girl to the bed and felt her sink down. How could she leave her in travail when no other help was at hand? On the other hand, what could she do in complete darkness?

"How often are the pains coming?"

"I'm not sure. Quite often."

"Not all the time, though? Would you say every fifteen minutes or so?"

"Perhaps…no…Oh, I don't know."

More sobbing and Hannah made a decision. "I am going to get out of here. You are going to be brave. I expect arrangements were made for you to come here. I don't know how it works but you've been sent here to have your baby; I am *not* having one…"

The girl interrupted. "Did you have an…you know, have they got rid of it? I was too late for that."

"How old are you? You sound very young."

"Sixteen."

The next twenty minutes were timeless for Hannah as the pair sat side by side on the bed, the younger girl pouring out confidences. There were too many voices and footsteps from within the house to make safe an escape. She felt almost hysterical with frustration and fear. At any moment someone might discover or recall the unlocked door and remember her presence behind it, on the other hand she dare not risk opening it until all was quiet.

At last sounds subsided. "Now, remember, be brave and don't make a sound when I open the door."

The lamp standing on a small table gave enough light for her to see the head of the stairs leading down to the tiled hall.

Audible now were whispers coming from the room next door and groans from the attics above. Treading softly and with the utmost care, her head a constant ball of pain and her thoughts unclear, Hannah stood for a moment peering below. A movement in the shadows caught her attention and she drew back, her heart jumping in her chest. Then came the sound of a key turning softly and she was sure the front door was opened. A draught of glacial air confirmed it. Someone was leaving the house.

Waiting until she heard it closing, she crept down the stairs and ran on tiptoe to the door, afraid now that she and everyone else might be locked inside. No, the door opened onto a scene of perfect stillness, the moonlight and the snow at the same time revealing the dreary street but masking its dinginess.

Footprints showed in fresh snow. Two sets, one small and narrow, leading to the house from the street where, judging by the churned snow a small horse-drawn vehicle had turned, and the other away from it. The small narrow set must belong to the girl in labour and the other larger ones to whoever had just left the building. Hannah waited for what she reckoned was a full two minutes then placing her boots in the most recently made prints walked into the street, brushing against the holly hedge. Her head seemed to clear in the cold air, pain remained from the blow received earlier, but her thoughts were sharp edged and possessed clarity.

A dumpy figure holding a large bag reminiscent of one seen weeks ago, had almost reached the end of the street and keeping to the shadows Hannah followed. Her instinct was to put a distance between herself and Blackfriar's Lane or to hide until merciful daylight made it safer to make her way to the apothecary shop which was a few streets away, but after hours spent as a prisoner compelled to listen to screams, moans and sinister whispers, she *had* to know what the woman was doing. She would inform Dr Lisle who had seemed ready, even eager, to be involved.

Glancing constantly backwards to be sure she was not being followed, she stayed a good one hundred yards behind the sturdy figure who reached the main street, empty except for a few huddled vagrants resembling heaps of rags as they sheltered in doorways. With quickened steps the woman crossed the main thoroughfare and disappeared down a sloping alley, a stinking ginnel where dirty snow lay thinly, lying between shops and leading towards the polluted waters of the Irwell where industrial and human waste created a noxious stew.

The ginnel opened onto a wide steeply sloping bank and by the time Hannah reached it, the woman was standing a foot or two from the slow-moving sludge. Keeping well back in shadow she watched as the bulky bag was opened and gasped involuntarily as the woman turned it over and let the contents fall with a soft splash into the filth below.

It might have been a doll, a naked white doll, pale in the moonlight, but it wasn't. Oh, God, it wasn't. Vomit rose in Hannah's throat and turning she put a hand to her mouth and blundered back along the alley, aware that the woman, her grim task completed, would be hurrying from the scene and closing the gap between them.

Her boots slipped on snow and muck, and she was panting and sobbing with a mixture of revulsion and terror when she reached the main street. To cross it might bring her to the attention of the solid figure whose dull footsteps could be heard and instinctively she hurled herself into a shop doorway where she lay, her cloak over her face, her hands wet with fear and a pulse throbbing in her temple.

The footsteps came closer and for one horrifying moment Hannah thought they had halted nearby, but risking a quick glance above folds of dark woollen material, she saw the woman crossing the street again, presumably retracing her steps. But safety was elusive. By now she may well have been missed and someone, maybe her abductor, could be scouring the streets and if he found her…her thoughts shied from a terrifying prospect. Might she too become a corpse sinking beneath murky waters?

She lay and considered and heard a distant clock striking four times. Too early for the factory workers to swarm along the street, and shops would not open for hours. Alone she was vulnerable, an easy target if she walked the streets. *Keeping to shadows is becoming a habit. Keeping company, even with some poor malodorous creature who sleeps in a doorway might offer a modicum of safety.* So ran her thoughts as she rose and pulled her cloak over her head before walking close to the walls and shop fronts seeking a strange kind of sanctuary.

A bundle of rags in the doorway of a drapery store stirred and Hannah caught a glimpse of a haggard female face whilst the smell of stale alcohol and unwashed flesh caught in her throat. She did not hesitate but stepped over the restless figure and slid in close beside her, willing herself to fight the overwhelming sickness that threatened. The vagrant moved restlessly, pushing Hannah who, lying against the shop door, cowered behind her and waited for the hours to pass.

The sound of horses' hooves echoed in the pre-dawn stillness and the noise of wheels heavier than those of a brougham drew closer. A brewer's dray? Whatever the heavy vehicle might be, more than one horse pulled it. Proceeding at a slow, almost leisurely pace, it came along the main street and risking a glance over the alcohol-soaked figure beside her, Hannah saw a carriage with lanterns and seated at the front were two men, one the driver with whip in hand. There was no way of knowing if the other was her abductor because she had not previously seen his face, but this man sought for someone, for some movement, his head turning from side to side as his gaze raked the shop fronts and the shadows that lurked between the gaslights. Despite the size of the carriage it moved with slow deliberation and she buried her face in the stinking rags beside her and held her breath.

It was gone, swallowed into the gloom, but still she lay until the factory sirens sounded and the street was alive with people and clatter, coughing, mutterings, the odd raised voice, a tide of weary down-trodden people; parents carrying tired children to their ten-hour shifts in the cotton mills, boots slithering on wet snow. Then she stepped over the motionless inebriate and fled along the main street, aware of places on her body that stung and itched – flea bitten, she guessed.

Old Mr Lawson stood behind the long counter in his shop and Hannah hammered on the door to attract his attention. He was early today; Sam usually opened the premises and got down to work, fulfilling orders, mixing and pounding, measuring and filling small blue, green and white bottles. She knew that those with ridges held poison but recalled her father telling her that many medicines contained what he believed were very dangerous substances, adding that even nature's own remedies might kill if taken in excess. Foxglove, aconite and belladonna for a start. How strange that she should think of it now, but perhaps not, when danger lurked on every side.

"Miss Morley! My dear young lady! Whatever…?" She pushed past him and crawled behind the counter.

"Sam? Where's Sam?" she heard her voice, weak and wavering.

"Young Samuel is detained at home. His father has taken a turn for the worse. This year's influenza is fickle. Tell me, what has happened? Something quite appalling, I fear."

"Mr Lawson, help me. I have to get word to Dr Marcus Lisle, and hide me, please." She got no further but sunk into unconsciousness.

*****

It seemed that she rose from gloomy depths and for a terrifying moment Hannah believed she was rising from the waters of the Irwell, but when she was fully awake discovered she was in a neat room containing two iron-framed beds heaped with blankets. A wicker chair and chest of drawers completed the furnishings and on the latter stood an oil lamp, unlit because clear bright light flooded into a room she did not recognise. Not Eliza Webster's, but whose?

Her exploring hands felt the roughness of the sheets but they smelled fresh and beneath them her bare legs and feet stretched. Her dress and stockings had been removed but she still had on her drawers and chemise.

The door opened and relief coursed through her as she recognised Mrs Stannard. So, she was in the workhouse. She attempted a smile but her face was painfully stiff and her head ached dully.

"My dear, whatever happened? No, I mustn't ask. You need rest because you have suffered some dreadful ordeal. I shall bring you a warm drink. Tea, hot chocolate, maybe? I have some in my room."

She hurried out but the door had hardly closed when it reopened and Dr Lisle's dark head appeared. "Are you fit to talk, Hannah?"

"I can try. My face and head hurt."

"I examined the injuries whilst you lay under Mr Lawson's counter. He sent for me. Bruising, bleeding and swelling. How did you come by them?" He drew the wicker chair closer to the bed and sat down.

"I was abducted, pushed into a carriage and hit across the face and head. My assailant was a gentleman. Believe that if you will, Dr Lisle."

"That is one thing he was not."

"He spoke with an educated accent, he smelt of expensive cologne or pomade, and he had a fob watch, well a chain, anyway. Not that I could see it but my fingers caught in it. I'll tell you the whole story, of course I will, but there's a very young girl in jeopardy in the house next to Mrs Wilson's. You know, at Next-Door-Nellie's."

"I told you to keep away." He sounded furiously angry.

"I was taken there. Oh, here's Mrs Stannard."

"And just in time, I'd say. Miss Morley is in no state to be harangued," came that woman's scolding tone as the doctor rose from the chair. She placed a mug of fragrant steaming chocolate on a bedside table and heaved Hannah up the bed, exposing her bare arms and revealing clusters of spots within areas of redness.

"Fleabites if I'm not mistaken. Oh, for goodness' sake, Hannah. Don't get coy with me," as she tried to snuggle down again. "I am well used to seeing arms, legs and everything else. May I suggest Mrs Stannard remains whilst you tell us your story"

"When she's had her chocolate and not before." The mug was pushed under Hannah's nose and the matron sat on the end of the bed. "Do sit down, doctor. This is no time to stand on ceremony."

With careful attention to detail, Hannah relived the terrors of the previous night and when she spoke in quiet jerky tones of the disposal of the small white body in the sulphurous waters of the river, Mrs Stannard's blue eyes opened wide with horror and shock.

"So they killed the baby?" she said breathily.

"I don't know," whispered Hannah. "I heard the cry of a new-born infant which grew stronger and then, nothing. It was cut off. And something awful was happening the other side of the wall; groans, whimpers and panicky whispers, and then there was the girl who was pushed in with me…she talked a lot, about her family finding somewhere for her to have the baby. It could be farmed out, she said, if a fee was paid and regular payments agreed. She seemed to think pregnancies could be terminated, again for a fee."

"She's almost certainly correct but a successful prosecution is hard to come by. And even if a baby's body is dredged up, we cannot prove conclusively how the death occurred, and if we did who was the perpetrator."

"It's all hopeless," Hannah felt a sob breaking and Dr Lisle took her hand.

"Perhaps not. Leave this to me, and Mrs Stannard…may I suggest Hannah is provided with a hot bath and a zinc oxide salve to stop the itch of those nasty bites."

"Of course. I have just the thing." She turned to Hannah. "We shall bring a bath and hot water and clean clothes, although you may wish to remain in bed for a while. This is the room you are to share with Sairin Williams; you remember, don't you? Later, Mr Gidley will speak with you."

Clean again, hair washed and nails scrubbed, Hannah thought with gratitude of the drink sodden rough sleeper who may unknowingly have saved her life. Wearing clothes and shawl lent by the matron, she left the room and walked across one of the exercise yards, empty owing to the snow underfoot and the piercing wind, and entered the main building.

Agnes Blair accosted her, the self-appointed housekeeper agog with news; bad news as usual which seemed to fascinate and she thrived on the telling. "Aye, it's a sad auld world. The carter wis here. Tells me another wee bairn found in the river. I daresay folk cannae afford a funeral so they rid themselves o' the burden like it wis rubbish. No' the first time and no' the last. Agnes kens it weel."

"Where?" Hannah asked sharply. "Where did this happen?" Agnes seemed to look at her properly for the first time.

"In the name o' goodness, lassie, what you been up tae?"

"I was attacked, but I'm all right. Tell me, where was the baby found?"

"Less than a mile frae the centre o' the city. Doon by the big mill. Attacked were ye? Puir lassie. It's a wicked world, so it is. I ken that weel."

It could be connected, thought Hannah. *That little body could be the one I saw dumped last night.*

"Ye look awfie bad. Where were ye attacked? Near here, wis it?"

"That's right, Agnes. Now I must hurry so excuse me." She wasn't going to give away too much information.

Mr Gidley greeted her with concern and kindness. "My dear lass, come in, sit down and rest awhile. Mrs Stannard has told me everything and it is shocking, quite terrible. The doctor has gone to make further investigations. Acquainted with a few men in our police service, so he says. Now, come to the fire."

He was like a kind old mother hen, thought Hannah and liked him the better for it. Unless she was very mistaken, he was good to the core.

Seated behind his desk once more, he reached for the leather-bound volume he had unearthed a day or so earlier, the early records of the past decade. "I'm rather proud of my detective work, Miss Morley. He pulled a marker from the pages and opened at an entry recorded ten years earlier."

"I invite you to read this." There was an edge of excitement in his voice. He pushed the oversized book across the desk and she lifted it onto her knee. "See here, Admissions. Go on, read it aloud and you'll see what I'm getting at."

Hannah glanced at the entry which held no particular meaning.

17th October, 1850. At six o'clock in the evening admitted by the porter, mother and daughter. The woman in poor physical condition after sleeping rough for some time in farm barns and hedgerows. Name given as Helena Rae. Age 22.

18th October, 1850 Death – Helena Rae aged 22. Admitted previous day. Died 4 o'clock in the morning.

Admission: Leah Rae, aged 2. No known living relatives. Placed in children's ward.

"I may seem very dull, Mr Gidley, but for the life of me I cannot make sense of this."

"Read it aloud, lass. Read the last bit aloud." He stood up and came around from behind the desk.

"Leah Rae! Don't you see? This could be the child Leary!"

****

Chapter Seventeen

"Good heavens! You could be right. How extraordinary and how clever of you, Mr Gidley."

"I could be wrong, but the age may be right and Leary, the girl you call Rosa, appears older than she believes herself to be and has known no other home but the workhouse. Of course, I may be jumping to conclusions."

"It feels right though, doesn't it? I think you may very well be correct it but it doesn't tell us why someone tried to abduct the girl. Unless it is because she is attractive and therefore vulnerable to the attentions of evil-minded men and women."

"Quite, quite. Well, we shall see. Meantime, a few of the women are minding your class and that of Miss Phipps until you are recovered. May I suggest you rest as much as possible after your ordeal? We can rely on the doctor to make all necessary enquiries."

*****

Hannah lay on the bed in the room she was to share with the Welsh girl and slept on and off as the bright light of day gave way to the dimness of fading light and finally darkness. At some point someone had entered the room and covered her with a light woollen blanket, and she awoke refreshed and strengthened, her aching head considerably improved.

A rapping on the door brought her fully awake and Agnes Blair put her head around it. "Carter's brought your bits and pieces, lassie. Yer baggage is oot here. Attacked, were ye?"

"I told you, Agnes. Yes, a nasty man hit me." It was like speaking to a young child and now that she was beginning to know the old woman better, she realised that at times her mind worked in the same way. Then, another thought crossed her mind. "Have you been here a long time? Did you ever know a child named Leah Rae?"

A strange haunted expression flickered across the lined features followed by one of puzzlement.

"I ken the name, leastways I think I dae, but I have nae been here for long years if that's whit ye mean. I wis appointed housekeeper," she ended proudly and Hannah knew the conversation had entered the realms of fantasy.

Later, having dragged her trunk into the room, she tidied her hair pulling the glossy dark strands into a smooth knot, patted the creases from a blue woollen dress and wrapped a shawl around her shoulders before walking across to the main building where girls and women had gathered for their evening meal. Feeling hungry, she sat with her class and having momentarily forgotten her bruised and swollen face, was startled by a number of stares, both interested and sympathetic.

"Did you fall, miss?" This from Fran Noone, and Hannah decided a brief version of the truth was required because rumours were bound to circulate.

"I was attacked by a ruffian when on my way home."

"Pity it wasn't Miss Phipps," remarked one of her class and some of the girls hid smiles and peeked at one another to gauge reactions to such a daring comment.

"She's still ill," went on Fran, "and she'll be mad as a caged rat when she gets back. Those women who took over today went through the cupboard and looked at her things. And we've used up all the paper that guardian brought us. Mind you, she didn't care when he took our work to look at it. We know what her name is. It's Martha!" Fran looked at Hannah. "Martha Phipps, 'orrible, en't it?"

"It's no worse than most," was the murmured reply as Hannah decided that she must restore order the next day no matter how she felt. She must also make contact with the Websters and write to her mother. Tiredness swept over her; it would take a while to recover and there seemed too much to do.

Following a meal of broth thickened with barley, and additional milk for the younger children, Mrs Stannard signalled that Hannah was to accompany her to Mr Gidley's office where Dr Lisle stood in front of the log fire, lines of weariness on his face, his shoulders drooping. Her heart went out to him and her smile was sympathetic.

He moved from the heat and she and Mrs Stannard seated themselves in the chairs he indicated. Mr Gidley entered, less ebullient than usual, his expression one of concentrated concern. Seated behind his desk he seemed diminished in some way, an air of unaccustomed gloom surrounding him.

"Ladies, the doctor here has told me a harrowing tale. Miss Morley has already played a part in it and been through the mill herself, so to speak. We're going to put our heads together and pool our knowledge, isn't that right, Dr Lisle? Though I fail to see how this place has a connection with what's the name... Blackfrairs something or other."

Dr Lisle took a deep breath and leaned back in the chair he had taken. "Let's remind ourselves briefly and then I'll inform you of today's events. Following Hannah's night of terror and subsequent adventures...not least hiding behind a flea infested, drink sodden rough sleeper...and her merciful escape, I visited the house accompanied by an acquaintance who is in the police service." Hannah leaned forward, eager to catch every word. "I required a reliable witness and who better?

"What did you find?" She was unable to restrain herself. "Did you get Nellie and the others?"

"We didn't get anyone, except a poor young girl, alone and in the last stages of labour. She'll be cared for and the child." He answered her unspoken question, adding, "Her testimony will be useful. The others appeared to have left. We searched and made some distressing discoveries. I fear someone may have suffered a severe blood loss last evening. There were indications of cleaning, some scrubbing and mopping, maybe, but the haemorrhage had obviously been considerable and cracks in the floorboards bore testimony. I am sorry, ladies."

Mrs Stannard bridled. "Dr Lisle, as a medical man, you must be aware that women are made of sterner stuff than most men give us credit for, and without wishing to be indelicate you will know that we are more familiar with the sight of..."

Poor Mr Gidley is the colour of a ripe plum, thought Hannah and felt very sorry for him. "What may have happened to the woman I heard in labour and the one who almost certainly haemorrhaged?" she asked quickly. "Were they whisked away? They'd be in no state."

"Carried into a carriage that waited outside, is my guess. There were a lot of footprints and scuffles in the snow. Think back, Hannah, to the night of thick fog when a vehicle waited. What exactly happened that night?"

"Not much. There was an air of controlled haste, of urgency." She tried to visualise the scene again, the sense of alarm experienced, the compelling need to make sure she remained invisible.

"I think someone said, 'Get her in,' and then, 'Lift her up.'"

"Did you hear a woman's voice?

"Sounds were muffled so I wasn't sure, but those words were definitely spoken by a man."

"So, someone unconscious or even dead might have been pushed into the carriage."

"That's absolutely horrible, but I suppose so." Despite the heat of the fire, she shuddered.

Dr Lisle's shapely hands gesticulated as he said, "Here is what I think has been happening. The woman Nellie and her accomplice, probably the uncouth person you talked about earlier, have been running an illegal business. You've heard what happened today but there has to be more. Possibly some babies were farmed out and a few enquiries may solve *that* mystery, but what if no-one was willing to pay for a child's upkeep? What if no-one was to profit?"

He left the question hanging in the air and Mr Gidley mopped his brow with a large handkerchief that had seen better days. "It happens, we know it does," he murmured unhappily.

"So Sal may have blurted out the truth. She *had* seen something," whispered Hannah, visions of a rough hand placed over a tiny mouth or pressure applied to a fragile neck. Unspeakable images filled her mind. Mrs Stannard, so bold a few moments before, looked sick. Mr Gidley now clasped his hands together as if in prayer.

"I am sure she did. Then there were times you and your mother saw the child in the backyard, obviously whilst things were happening in the house. I suspect she became a danger, maybe tried to escape and was followed. I don't suppose we shall ever know."

"Any more than we know who she was or how long she had been there," remarked Mrs Stannard. "I doubt she was a workhouse child; why would women involved in their line of business risk taking in a child and having her about the place?"

"She may have been the natural child of one of the women, but who inflicted the fatal injury we may never know. But we shall find the women, be sure of that." There was silence for a full half minute broken by Hannah.

"Maybe the woman I glimpsed at Sal's funeral was her natural mother..." she mused before turning to the master. "Let us tell the others about your detection work, Mr Gidley. About Rosa, that is Leary, and how that isn't her name at all."

"Whoa! Think on, Miss Morley. We shall all be in a fine muddle if we go too fast. It's this way, we have been trying to discover something of the other child's past and I may have stumbled on something." His tone was self-deprecating. "Though, I could be fooling myself and Miss Morley too."

"Well, don't tease us, Mr Gidley," Mrs Stannard sounded almost light-hearted and Hannah noticed the fond look she cast in his direction.

"Have a look for yourselves." He unearthed the records of ten years earlier, and she and the doctor pored over the relevant page.

"Well, I never did! It seems possible to me. You are very clever, Mr Gidley. Very clever indeed. What do you say, Dr Lisle?"

"It needs some thought, but it is possible. I believe there's a prominent local family who own an estate some miles off and have another fine place further north. Not Rae, but something like it. Yes, got it! Stuart-Rae."

"Are you suggesting there's a connection, doctor? It seems highly unlikely." The matron glanced sharply at him.

"Apologies, I digress. I recall the name only because the elderly landowner was killed whilst out hunting a year or so ago. I recall Mr Meredith mentioning it."

"*He* should know, he moves in such circles, I am told." Mrs Stannard's tone was dry and disapproving.

Hannah gave a deep sigh and attention focussed on her again. "What worries me is that I am sure I was abducted because of a connection with Rosa. The man kept asking me for her whereabouts. It's Rosa they want, whoever they are; but why was *I* taken to Next-Door-Nellie?"

"Could it be we've all been missing the point? Oh, dear me." Mr Gidley's handkerchief was in use again.

"There's something else." Hannah looked around at the company. "After the blow to my head, I said the first thing that came to mind when asked about Rosa. I lied and said she was staying near Longwell. That's where my mother is and I'm very afraid for her. She may be in danger. I need to see her. In fact, I must."

****

Chapter Eighteen

"Tomorrow morning, Elias Williams will take you to Longwell," Mrs Stannard announced later. "He is in a hurry to collect materials from someone out that way. I don't know the ins and outs of it, but we are lending him a horse and trap, and if you accompany him you may spend an hour or two with your mother and your mind will be eased. Sairin, his daughter, will be with him."

It was later when she entered the bedroom that she met the attractive twelve-year-old, a slight child with whom conversation was difficult. Her shyness was crippling and Hannah felt it kinder to refrain from questions, so busied herself brushing her hair and preparing for bed before huddling beneath a pile of blankets. If the child noticed Hannah's bruised face, she made no comment.

The following morning, her early duties completed and the classes of girls once more in the dubious care of two respectable but uneducated women inmates, she dressed in a warm woollen gown and cloak, pulled on a bonnet and waited with Sairin for the trap to arrive at the main door. In her reticule was money from her first month's earnings and she would see that Mrs Mariah Simpson was reimbursed for the hospitality shown to Belle.

Sairin was slightly less withdrawn and very warmly clad in a tweed outfit her father had made with expert skill. The girl must have found the workhouse environment strange. She knew no one but her father and back in Ruthin her mother was ill, mortally so, Mrs Stannard hinted. Hannah felt pity for her and gently encouraged a light-hearted conversation until the pony and trap appeared, Mr Williams smiling fondly upon his daughter and inviting Hannah to "Climb aboard, now. Room for the three of us, isn't it? Thank the good Lord for a fine day. I've bolts of material to collect. Not waiting for a delivery." His speech was staccato and Hannah wondered whether his first language was Welsh and when he thought in English the sentences became shortened.

It was cold and clear, remaining snow frozen at the roadside as they left behind the smoke of factories and the busy streets; driving through suburbs where large houses were being built and trees planted along newly created avenues and wide roads. The little trap bounced along and soon they were into the countryside. Hannah's spirits lifted as a skein of noisy cackling geese flew overhead on their way to winter-feeding grounds.

"There's beautiful," Elias Williams said. "Lovely and free they are." He sighed, and Hannah imagined he was thinking of his poor wife, trapped by illness. Not for her the touch of cold refreshing winter air, the sight of frosted fields, the call of birds and the sight of cottages where hens pecked beside the door and cats curled on window sills.

"Will you get home before long?" Hannah asked, hoping the question was not impertinent or inappropriate in the circumstances.

"Savin' my time off. Sairin and me, we'll be off for a few days when I've got on with things, see? New uniforms to be made. New assistants to train." He looked down at his daughter. "Your Mam's ill, isn't she cariad? Being nursed by Bethan and Nain. That's her grandmother, Miss Morley."

Seeing Sairin on the point of tears, Hannah hastily pointed out lads in a field trying unsuccessfully to halter a lively brown horse.

"You'll 'ave three hours with your Mam; we'll be back mid-afternoon, see." Elias told her as they entered Longwell and Hannah felt like hugging him. "Pretty place; be lovely in summer."

Seeing it with fresh eyes, Hannah agreed with him wholeheartedly. After the soot and grime of the city, sulphurous fogs and polluted waters, Longwell appeared clean-swept by winds from the moorland. The snow lying in ditches and gardens appeared unsullied and even that trodden and crushed on the road was marked only by good honest muck and mud, as they said hereabouts.

Mrs Simpson's welcome left nothing to be desired. Her kind face beamed as her firm hands pulled Hannah into her modest little home where brasses twinkled and a fire burned in the living room hearth. She whispered, "What happened to your poor face?"

"A fall in the snow. Mama must not be upset. Let's make light of it." The other woman nodded.

"See who's here, Belle," she exclaimed and Hannah's mother gave a cry of joy, leaping from a comfortable tapestry covered chair that was too large for her, and embracing her with warmth.

"What a surprise! Only this morning I said to Mariah that I longed for a glimpse of your face; but whatever has happened? Such nasty bruises." Hannah repeated the lie.

"Oh, my dear, how dreadful, but here you are as if by magic."

"By pony and trap! I shall be collected in the mid-afternoon. You look well, Mama. Well and happy."

"Your mother is in her element. Let me have your bonnet and cloak, my dear, and I shall make you a hot drink. Lunch is lamb stew and dumplings, and we have some leftover apple pie. We used the last of the stored apples, didn't we, Belle? You are a tonic, Hannah, believe me."

She left them together and for a moment they were enveloped in silence, then both spoke together. "You first, Mama," invited Hannah as her mother sat down and she seated herself in a wooden rocking chair made soft with cushions encased in red knitted covers.

"I missed this kind of thing so much, Hannah. You should have seen the candles and the greenery in the church on Christmas day. To think we live in that frightful attic room. Why do we?"

"Not anymore; we shall move, but you know why, Mama. Our money was disappearing fast. Perhaps I was too careful and we might have taken better rooms. We will now I'm working and meantime I have money here for Mrs Simpson." At that moment the woman hurried in with a china mug brimming with tea and handed it to Hannah before withdrawing quickly.

Belle fidgeted with the mourning brooch at her throat. "It may seem very ungrateful, my dear, but Mariah has hinted that she would like me to stay here. We get along very well, but it isn't just that. She gets nervous living by herself and the last two days have been rather nerve-wracking."

"What do you mean, Mama? What's happened?" Hannah's tone was sharp and agitated.

"Nothing has actually happened. But you know what a village is like. Any unknown face arouses interest and there *have* been a couple of strangers around. I mean, why should they wish to visit a place like this in the dead of winter? Besides, they've been asking questions."

"Luncheon is served in the kitchen because it is warm in there. Oh, is something amiss?" Mariah coming into the room again glanced from one to the other in consternation.

Belle adjusted her black dress and rose to her feet. "I was telling Hannah about the strangers in our midst. It's a mystery but no doubt they will leave. "She gave an uneasy high-pitched laugh. "We can't find out where they are staying. Nobody seems to know."

Hannah's appetite disappeared despite the well-cooked meal placed before them on a kitchen table covered with a white damask cloth and served on painted china plates. In front of the black leaded range, an elderly ginger cat slept in a wicker basket lined with a frayed shawl. Figurines stood upon the mantle-piece and there was an air of modest prosperity about the place. Mama must so enjoy it. She would encourage the suggestion that she stay, possibly make her home with Mariah Simpson.

"What are these strangers like?" she managed as she played with pieces of tender meat that slid around her plate. "Have they threatened anyone?"

"Hannah! What a horrid thought. No, dear, they watch. Mariah thought they watched this house, didn't you, Mariah? Yesterday, that was. We drew the curtains early, and two of the village women called in to tell us that one of the men had enquired if we had a little girl staying with us.

"Nonsense, of course," Mariah said stoutly. "I don't keep a maid. A village girl comes in daily to do the rough work. Now. Hannah, eat up, dear. I never stint on food."

"What did the men look like?" she asked, her throat tight with fear. *What if Mama or Mrs Simpson was accosted, threatened, or worse, abducted, because it was believed they were hiding Rosa.*

"Don't upset yourself, Hannah. It is a storm in a teacup. There'll be looking for a runaway. Maybe from an asylum of some kind, an apprentice, or a girl from one of the farms or estates around here. And I wouldn't blame anyone for running away from one or two of them. From what I hear some servants would be better off in the workhouse." Mrs Simpson ladled more stew onto Belle's plate.

"Speaking of which, Mama, I am staying at what you refer to as *that place*. Mrs Wilson is no longer letting rooms. I spent two nights at the home of Sam Webster and his sister," she paused. "You recall Sam from the apothecary's, and then was offered accommodation at the workhouse?" Her mother would collapse and go into a decline if she heard the truth.

"*That place!*" Whatever are you thinking of, Hannah? It's bad enough you should be forced to work amongst the dregs of society without sharing a roof. What would your dear father have said?"

"I think he might have been proud of me. He was most unconventional, wasn't he? For a start you will recall that he told me never to go into deep mourning. If there was one thing he hated, it was women disguised as crows." *Oh dear, and there was Mama wearing unrelieved black.* To apologise would underline her gaffe. Blushing with confusion, she suggested that after luncheon they walk the few hundred yards to the old church so that she might see the seasonal decorations over which her mother had enthused.

"I insist you enjoy one another's company whilst I tidy here." Mariah was adamant. "Go while it is fine and bright, but be careful. It's treacherous underfoot. You'll need your sturdy boots, Belle."

"She is very thoughtful for my comfort," her mother said as they linked arms and emerged into the main street that ran between rows of low cottages before winding between older timber framed buildings, so haphazardly placed, they appeared to have grown out of the ground. "Of course, you are too, Hannah. No one could have a better daughter, but you understand, don't you? I belong here."

Hannah squeezed her arm. "Of course, Mama. It's been very difficult for you. I shall do very well in my work and it's safe in the workhouse."

"Have you been in danger? Has anything happened in my absence?" Her mother could be quite perceptive. *Oh, Mama, if only you knew but I shall never tell you the half of it.*

"I am perfectly safe. Here we are, Green Lane and the church. I used to love coming here for festivals and celebrations although I admit when the Reverend Lovatt-Browne was long winded, I studied the stained glass windows and counted the tiny panes of coloured glass."

"You were always a wayward child. So like your father, God rest him. I wish he was buried here. So much easier to visit than travelling to his birthplace."

Hannah held open the low wrought iron gate that led into the churchyard and Belle led the way along a wide path flanked by gravestones. The snow was well-trodden and wet where sunlight filtered between ancient yew trees and its stone paving was visible here and there. There were wet marks in the porch and Hannah wondered who else might have entered. Were they still within?

Inside the smell of green branches mingled with that of incense. Belle had not exaggerated the beauty of long ivy stems wound around ancient stone pillars and holly arranged around plump white candles set in niches and along sills. The altar was decked in lace cloths and brass candlesticks and to one side of it stood a manger scene, the infant Christ a china doll, no doubt loaned with pride by one of the village families. Hannah felt a longing for the old days, her childhood days, when life had seemed secure and happy, as if it might continue that way for ever.

Her mother was intent upon examining every artistic plant arrangement and Hannah wandered into the side chapel, a remnant of a building pre-dating the centuries old church, its window glass plain and a low narrow door, half hidden by a purple curtain, leading to the outside. Another smaller altar stood within and it too was decked in fine lace. It was as she stood admiring the stitch-work she became aware of a scent that filled her with alarm and her stomach tightened; beneath her bonnet the hairs on her head bristled. Expensive cologne. God help her! Was her abductor here in this place of sanctuary – this old church? Did she imagine that the purple door curtain billowed slightly? Frantically she gazed around before turning abruptly and stumbling into a side aisle, she hurried towards Belle.

"Are you all right, my dear? You look as if a goose walked over your grave."

"I am fine, Mama," she said loudly, praying that anyone listening might not know of her alarm and really, when one considered it, many men must favour the product. "But it is cold in here and I shall have to be going back soon. Oh!" she gasped as the main door was pushed open, "Oh! It is only the Reverend Lovatt-Browne, Mama."

"That sounds decidedly disrespectful to me," her mother murmured and hurried to greet the tall elderly cleric who stamped his feet and coughed as he entered. Although dressed in a loose tweed coat that reached his knees, he appeared cold to the bone. "Mr Lovatt-Browne," Belle almost fawned, "See, Hannah has come to visit."

"A delightful surprise, Miss Morley, and as you have been good enough to acquaint me with progress in your place of work, I feel I have a part in it."

She watched as a drop of moisture formed on the end of his aquiline nose and waited for its inevitable descent. "You so kindly wrote me a reference, sir; it is the least I can do. There are such changes and improvements at the workhouse."

"All to the good," he muttered vaguely, clutching the back of an oak pew for support. "I met one of your acquaintances earlier today, a gentleman of the medical profession, I believe. Interested in various family histories. I am afraid I was of little assistance but I may have pointed him in the right direction."

Dr Lisle? she wondered. If so, what had he been doing here? What too of the man who might even now be hidden in the building? The desire to run out of it was almost overwhelming.

"Such a joy to be back in the village," Belle was saying. "The church so beautifully decked and your Christmas sermon the best I have heard." *Oh, Mama, you are such a flatterer.*

Hannah thought the poor man was about to collapse as his grip tightened on the pew and his knuckles turned white. His frailty was apparent.

"It is very chilly and perhaps we should all be indoors," she suggested as a flow of icy air whirled around her ankles. Was that the sound of a door closing softly? Her nerves were stretched to breaking point so maybe she imagined it.

"Then, good day, ladies," said the cleric. "I shall bid you farewell. I have one or two matters to attend to within the church but soon I shall be back in the rectory and warmly ensconced in my fireside chair."

"We can easily wait and see you safely home," began Hannah, but he waved the suggestion aside impatiently.

"I may be getting on in years but I am not a helpless old fool, yet."

"It is impossible to help some people," remarked Belle as they clung to one another and walked from the church to the lane. "You'll be like that when you grow old, Hannah. Far too independent for your own good."

Hannah was not listening. Were they being observed? Potential menace seemed to lurk behind every yew and cracked uneven gravestone. It was unbearably difficult to act naturally and to refrain from scanning their surroundings. Presumably the man who wore cologne would remain hidden but she half expected to see a menacing cloaked *female* figure standing beside one of the dark yews. At that moment, the workhouse seemed the safest place on earth.

****

Chapter Nineteen

Elias Williams was anxious to make haste when he and Sairin returned with a trap laden with bolts of material and soon Hannah was spreading a blanket over Sairin and herself, waving to her mother and Mariah who stood at a mullioned window watching the departure.

The girl looked half-frozen and tired, and leaned wearily against Hannah, who put an arm around the thin shoulders and warmed her with her own body. After a while, Sairin slumped against her and slept.

"I shouldn't have brought her but she didn't want to be left in the house. Something about that woman Phipps asking her questions and making a nuisance of herself, so it is."

"Miss Phipps is ill, confined to bed. She fainted in class two or three days ago."

"Maybe, but she was up and about yesterday. Sairin was upset when the woman insisted on combing her hair. Lovely hair my Sairin has, fine as cobwebs, buttercup yellow. There, I go, sound like a poet, isn't it?"

A mental picture arose in Hannah's mind, Molly Tinsley and the teacher, the latter's hands entwined in a halo of fair hair. Girls with beautiful hair must hold an attraction for the strange Miss Phipps. She wondered whether her work was a result of it, an opportunity to be close to pretty young girls.

Did telepathy play a part she wondered when Mr Gidley sought her out after the early evening meal. Molly was on his mind too, but he beamed.

"Let me put your mind at rest, lass. The relieving officer was out Bolton way and called at the establishment. Most of the girls were at their duties but he saw three or four of them including Molly Tinsley. I have the report here: *a quiet girl but she appears in good health and spirits, well-nourished and clean, her dark hair washed and brushed.*"

"That's not right, Mr Gidley. Molly has very fair hair, like a halo, and Molly isn't quiet. She is bold."

"A slip, my dear. He had more than one girl to interview. There were other placements in other establishments. I think we can rest our minds."

"Well, I don't," Hannah said more briskly than intended. "Don't you see, Mr Gidley, we cannot be sure Molly is safe and well unless we know the relieving officer saw the right girl. I...I know I have experienced and seen the worst of human nature lately but I have to be certain."

"I suppose I could enquire of Mr Jasper Meredith. He is acquainted with the philanthropist who organises the training of these young women." The Master appeared agitated. "But I might appear to doubt his judgement. Leave it with me and I shall question the relieving officer again." He looked at Hannah with genuine concern. "The bruising is coming out on your poor face. Take it easy, lass."

The next day after morning lessons, Hannah walked to Chandler's Court. Eliza, pale and anxious, greeted her with concern. "Dr Lisle told us of your ordeal. You poor thing," she lisped, kindness in her pale eyes.

"How is your father?" enquired Hannah as they went upstairs to the apartment.

"Over this particular crisis, thank God. The doctor has been wonderfully attentive and Mr Lawson's let Sam leave his work early. Rosa is a godsend. She's not been outside; you know why, but she seems happy enough and can't get enough of the warmth. She clings to the range but no doubt she's felt cold most of her life."

Seated at the scrubbed table, Hannah too luxuriated in the cosiness of the Websters' kitchen as she sipped hot chocolate and ate fruitcake Rosa claimed to have baked. "She did too," said Eliza when the girl went to check on old Mr Webster. "She is a fast learner."

Quickly Hannah explained that Rosa was almost certainly older than she believed and brought her up to date with events in Longwell and in the workhouse. "It's just possible we have a record of her entry into the system and if so, she is twelve and her real name isn't Leary at all, but Leah Rae."

"Rae?" Eliza considered the name. "I think that's the surname of the man who is helping at the ragged school. Rae something, or something Rae. You remember, the journalist I told you about."

"Do you think he *is* a journalist? I've begun to doubt everybody and anything they tell me."

"Well, you can trust the Webster family," smiled Eliza, "but in answer to your question, I don't know. He asks about everything; he says he is writing about the poor and dispossessed, as he calls them – workhouse children, apprentices, factory workers, child labourers and so on. He asked about *my* circumstances so I told him I wasn't one of them! I didn't mention Rosa, you can be sure of that."

"You're a fine person, Eliza. One of the best. Are you willing to keep Rosa for a while?"

"Indeed I am. As I said, she is invaluable, but I am uneasy because someone is seeking her and determined to find her." Changing the subject, she mentioned that Sam would be sorry to have missed the visit. "He likes you, Hannah. He likes you very much."

"I like Sam too." Hannah hesitated feeling she should say more. "…I just hope he doesn't mistake my friendship for more than that, Eliza. I can't tell you how much I value him as a friend and appreciate all he has done but…"

"You don't need to explain. I know exactly how it is, believe me. I mean, one knows when it is more than that." She coloured. At that point Rosa came into the kitchen reminding Eliza that it was time for the patient's dinner.

"Time for me to go." Hannah rose and dropped a kiss on Rosa's dark head. "Thank you with all my heart, Eliza. For…everything."

"Would you like to accompany me to the nearby ragged school this evening?" Eliza asked quietly. "You've enough on your plate so not to help regularly, but to see what we do."

"I'd love to," Hannah told her truthfully. "Till tonight then."

*****

Her mother's letter was waiting for her when she arrived back at the workhouse. A special delivery she was informed. It was less than twenty-four hours since she had seen Mama but the meeting had reminded her of their closeness, thought Hannah indulgently.

Seated on the end of her bed, she opened the envelope and withdrew a flimsy piece of paper, her heart beating fast as she read and re-read her mother's neat script.

"...of course, my dear, we should not have left him alone. His frailty was obvious. To think he must have fallen and hit his poor head, almost certainly soon after our departure. One can only hope and pray his demise was quick and that he did not suffer. Believe me, the village is in a state of deep shock...

What a dreadful thing to happen. The Reverend Horatio Lovatt-Browne must have fallen, collapsed possibly, and died as a result of a head injury. Or...? With shaking hands Hannah pushed the letter back into the envelope as if she would hide from herself the knowledge of the gentle old man's death. Clearly she saw again, the church still decked with Christmas greenery, the innocent tableau of the manger scene, the fine altar cloths, and felt again the spiteful current of air whilst hearing the quiet closing of a door. Had an intruder left by the side chapel door and re-entered to accost the Reverend? Had the old gentleman taken a step backwards and fallen? Worse, had he been bullied and pushed?

Why, oh why, had she not remained for a while? She and Mama could have seated themselves quietly, unobtrusively, and waited.

The truth was she had been in a hurry to leave and not only because Elias Williams might appear with the pony and trap. She had fled from possible danger. True, she had not believed anyone but her mother and herself might be threatened at that moment, but even so...

Hannah sat with bowed head and the tears coursed down her cheeks. The Reverend Lovatt-Browne had been a good man, a part of her childhood, careful of his people, quiet and kind. The thoughts raced through her mind and one was predominant. It was because of Rosa – Leary – Leah Rae, whatever the child's real name might be, that this had happened.

Crossing to the washstand, she poured ice-cold water from the ewer into a small basin and dipping a cloth into it she wiped her face, then washed her hands before drying them on a rough towel.

Somehow she had to get through the rest of the day.

The relieving ward was busier than usual. Wintry weather brought in more accident cases, broken bones chiefly, then there were those with congestion of the lungs and two old men, rough-sleepers practically frozen to death. There was a girl, surely no more than seven or eight years old, whose crushed finger hung by a sliver of skin, injured as she crept beneath a spinning machine picking up the cotton fluff.

"The law forbids any as young as that to work in the factories but the owners turn a blind eye and so do the parents, desperate as they are for the pittance paid." Mrs Stannard examined the injury. "She'll lose the finger, and she's in shock which is dangerous. A blanket, Hannah, some laudanum… If only Dr Lisle was here but he is away for two or three days."

She had guessed it was he who had spoken to the now deceased Reverend Lovatt-Browne but he had not mentioned that he was visiting Longwell nor that he would be absent for a while. Absurdly she felt ruffled by the omission which showed he did not entirely trust her whilst she had trusted him entirely.

"Hannah, Miss Morley! Pay attention. A blanket, and be quick about it. The child is shivering. The children's hospital is woefully inadequate and so this poor child ends up here. Let's be sure it is not in vain." She hurried to and fro, her dark skirts rustling; examining, bandaging, dosing and calling instructions to Hannah and two women attendants whose assistance left much to be desired, and all the time a tide of pitiful humanity continued to sweep in.

Hannah was drained of energy by the end of a long afternoon but revived after a meal of barley broth and hunks of bread and cheese washed down by sweetened tea. Even so, she had overestimated her ability to recover quickly from recent events and had it been possible, she would have sent word to Eliza that she was unable to visit the ragged school. As it was, she felt compelled to keep to their arrangement and buffeted by a cruel wind, and with keen awareness lest she was followed, she walked on frozen pavements to the warehouse where the school was held.

Situated close to the banks of the river, the stink of the polluted water caught at the back of her throat and the noise of raised voices reached her long before she entered the chilly building to find crowds of young boys stuffing food into their mouths. Although the odour of unwashed bodies mingled with that of the hot baked potatoes being devoured, Hannah noticed that the garments worn by the children were far from being rags. Having observed her entrance, Eliza rushed to her side and explained.

"We take their filthy rags and for the time spent here they are clothed properly, but we *have* to send them home in what they wore or their parents would sell anything clean and decent." She put a hand to her mouth in an unconscious gesture that hid her cleft lip. "As you see, we have tables, donated by some of the local businessmen, and benches, but it is a case of food first and then lessons. We've been provided with slates and tonight we shall try and teach them their letters. You look tired, Hannah, but if you want to help, just talk with the lads; they like an interested adult. Most earn what they can during a twelve-hour day, some sweeping out stables, some making match boxes or selling matches on windy corners, or helping in some home industry…it's endless. Oh! Here is…" She blushed hotly. "The Reverend James Christie. You must be acquainted with him. He attends the workhouse. He's so interested in all we try to do here."

"Miss Morley, a pleasure to see you. Eliza…Miss Webster that is, good evening." His single-breasted coat was worn, his eyes tired and he too seemed flustered. "As I always say, you and your helpers are doing wonderful things here." Turning to Hannah he continued, "Some boys want to learn and most will pick up something, even if it is only to write their own names, but we are under no illusions that it is food and warmth they crave. We are planning overnight shelter for the little ones who sleep in doorways and ginnels, and already turn a blind eye to those who creep back in here."

"I brought down more blankets," Eliza said, her cheeks reddening again. "I knit strips and sew them together whilst I am sitting with Father."

"Wonderful! I shall call and pay my respects to him," James Christie said and a delighted smile tugged at Eliza's misshapen lips. "I see we have another visitor tonight. If I'm not mistaken, it's the journalist, Duncan Stuart-Rae."

Hannah swung round, her interest aroused at the name. The visitor cut an elegant figure in a thigh length coat bordered with fur, and was apparently unaware of the discrepancies between his attire and his surroundings. Could this man have a connection with Rosa? More to the point, what were his intentions? "Let me introduce you," the curate was saying, and she was soon shaking hands with this earnest looking man of middle years, his once black hair showing signs of grey. Did she imagine keen interest in his gaze, in the grey eyes that pinned her to the spot? Probably, but there was not the faintest whiff of cologne about him, she noted with relief.

"I am here to help when and if required," he told Hannah in a soft cultured voice that held the trace of an accent, "but mainly to observe and talk to the boys. Are you familiar with the novels of Mr Dickens, Miss Morley? I see you are; he does not exaggerate the sufferings of the poor as you are probably aware. Not possessing his immense talent, I cannot and would not try to emulate his creative writing, my aim is to prick the consciences of an educated readership. Some published writings may have already borne fruit, but in any event there are more initiatives now to help and support the poor – factory laws, asylums, industrial schools. You are a good listener, but I must not weary you with my meanderings."

"Far from it, Mr Stuart-Rae. I am employed at the workhouse and see so much that requires improvement in our society, although the new master and the guardians have a full rebuilding programme, we have better qualified staff and the matron, Mrs Stannard, is an excellent woman."

"Have you heard of an inmate named Agnes Blair?" he asked without hesitation.

"I know someone of that name," Hannah began carefully. "An elderly Scotswoman. She is a self-appointed housekeeper and a hard worker."

"Does she talk to you, perhaps speak of the past as old people do?"

"She is concerned about the unfairness of life and fixated on certain recent tragedies, but is muddled at times and no, she has not spoken of her past to me."

It was on the tip of her tongue to ask if the name Helena Rae meant anything to him but instead she suggested they attempt to control the boys who having eaten were milling about looking for trouble, or maybe just attention.

Her tiredness forgotten, Hannah entered into the spirit of the evening sessions, talking to the young boys, helping them with their work, and telling small groups of them stories and legends to which they listened with flattering attention.

"You transported them to other worlds, Miss Morley. You have a talent for creating pictures from mere words." The Reverend James Christie was at her side.

"I could say the same about you," she told him, but she no longer had his full attention. He was looking at Eliza who was washing and cutting a boy's unkempt and shaggy hair.

"She's a special person," Hannah said softly. "Pure gold, wouldn't you say? I think she could do with your help, Mr Christie."

"Do you really? Well, maybe…" He was gone, his long strides taking him swiftly to Eliza who glanced at him with tenderness. *Matchmaker!* Hannah told herself, but it would be charming if those two good people fell in love, and unless she was mistaken, they were half way to doing that already.

It was as she walked back to her workhouse lodgings that she pondered on the conversation with Mr Duncan Stuart-Rae. Why his interest in old Agnes Blair? She should have asked him bluntly and now the opportunity had passed. A while later as she entered the main building and caught sight of the woman herself, something clicked in her mind. Agnes had been housekeeper for a prominent family. What if that family had been Stuart-Rae? What if Helena Rae had been a daughter of the house and had somehow ended in the workhouse; and why was Agnes here? She was competent enough, just slightly muddled as if her mind had been turned. Her thoughts fell over one another as she rushed after the sturdy figure now ascending the wide stone stairs and singing softly to herself.

"Mrs Blair…Agnes, please wait, I want to ask you something." The woman turned and seeing Hannah, smiled broadly.

"Dinnae fash yoursel'. I'm no goin' anywhere. Yer bruises are nae worse, that's a mercy."

"Agnes, please think carefully. Do you know a family called Stuart-Rae?"

"I'm nae saying a thing. I dinnae ken whit ye mean?"

"Agnes, please. There's a little girl at risk. A child I think may be called Leah Rae. Does the name mean anything to you?"

"I dinnae ken the name. But oh, my puir lasssie; they'd hae put her awa' but auld Agnes fooled the lot o' them."

It was impossible to make sense of what the muddled woman said. Hannah tried again. "Agnes, think carefully. Did you ever know a woman named Helena Rae?"

She was completely unprepared for Agnes's reaction. The woman's plump face seemed to sag and colour drained from her puffy cheeks before terror peeped out of her eyes. "Dinnae say the name. It's nae permitted. The master'll put me in the asylum for the mad folks, so he will."

"Helena died, Agnes. Ten years ago. Nobody is going to hurt you. Mr Gidley isn't going to put you in an asylum. You're safe here."

"Get awa' frae me this very minute. I dinnae ken anyone and that's a fact." With her face contorted with panic and fear, Agnes turned and rushed away, leaving Hannah staring after her in alarm.

****

Chapter Twenty

The Reverend James Christie appeared tired when next he visited the workhouse and no wonder, thought Hannah. There was little spare time for a curate whose lot was to perform many thankless tasks within the parish but he seemed to take pleasure in the chaplaincy of the workhouse. She wondered whether New Year's Day, falling on a Sunday, would concentrate some duties and possibly give him time to spend with the Websters. Yes, he had visited, he informed her, as he rubbed together cold hands in an effort to warm them. She fancied Eliza might enjoy knitting him a pair of woollen mittens.

"Eliza's father is improved in health but she carries a burden. The old man is frail. However, Eliza has inner strength." It occurred to Hannah that in common with most people who were more than half way to being in love, there was a compulsion to mention the beloved's name. She smiled encouragingly.

"I am exceedingly impressed with the work she does at the ragged school. You are often there, I gather."

"I try to do my bit. We have more helpers now and Mr Stuart-Rae is to publish a piece about our work, that is about our particular school, in the near future. He seems both concerned and able, wouldn't you say?"

"Concerned, yes, but I'm not sure that I have read any of his work. He aims to stir consciences, I believe. He didn't say so but I imagine if tender consciences mean people of means dipped into their financial resources and wrote cheques to benefit the ragged school, it's all to the good."

"Indeed, but as Eliza reminds me, one needs to get a conversation going. She wants readers to talk about the all too often hidden work undertaken. Wouldn't you say she combines the qualities of both Mary and Martha as they feature in the Scriptures? The mindfulness of one and the practical capabilities of the other?"

"Oh, I would, Mr Christie. I hope you have told her. My feeling is Eliza lacks confidence but with the right friends about her, she will blossom like the rose."

"Poetically expressed," Miss Morley. "Like the rose…quite so."

Was it too much to hope that the curate might be bold enough to send Eliza a St Valentine's card containing a verse or two about *her* rose-like complexion? Theirs was a romance waiting to happen if she was reading the signs aright.

*****

Dr Marcus Lisle returned the following day, appearing during the afternoon session on the relieving ward. Hannah had intended to greet his return with a certain coolness but looking up from the injured foot of a young boy who had trodden on a field rake and pierced the sole, she found herself smiling warmly. After a word with Mrs Stannard, he crossed to her side.

"I have news concerning Rosa," he said quietly.

She nodded. "I have news too. The Reverend Lovatt-Browne was found dead in Longwell Church. It must have happened soon after my mother and I left the building."

A shadow crossed his features. "That is dreadful. Natural causes? An accident?"

"I don't know; I'm not sure anyone does. My mother wrote immediately she heard of it."

"I spoke with him. He was frail and the uncomfortable rectory full of malicious draughts. Even the fire would not draw. A courageous man in his own way," he said as Hannah bent over the injured foot again, "and I am very sorry to hear of his death. We cannot talk here but are to meet in the master's office."

Mr Gidley welcomed them and the matron with his usual warmth. "Be seated, everyone. Come close to the fire. So, where are we?" he asked, rubbing his hands together. "You, Dr Lisle have been investigating, so may I suggest you share your findings."

"I believe I have discovered something of Rosa's history. It was the name Rae that set me on the right track, and that's thanks to your research, Mr Gidley." He nodded in the master's direction. "I wished to be sure of certain facts and made a visit to the rector of Longwell because he has long been acquainted with families, both notable and less so, in that area. He informed me that a daughter of the Stuart-Rae family died away from home some twelve years ago. He did not officiate at her funeral. The dates did not tie up with your records."

"How intriguing." The matron leaned forward. "This is like a novel." Dr Lisle ignored the comment. "He gave me a letter of introduction to Lady Stuart-Rae, the widow of the late baronet who was killed whilst hunting. I found her a very poor soul, not old but worn with sorrow."

"To lose a beloved spouse..." began Mrs Stannard, although her glance rested on Mr Gidley as she spoke, "...an appalling loss."

"Frankly, I don't think she gave a damn about him, begging your pardon, ladies. He was a dictator, a bully, an autocrat whose will was law. How could any woman love such a man? No, she has mourned the loss of her daughter. I heard the story, unwittingly implied by the rector. Let me try to give an impression of the lady and tell the story in her words. She is small and nervous, dressed in unrelieved black as is the custom but I have the notion she may have worn mourning for years. Now that the burden of a tyrannical husband is lifted, she seemed eager to talk."

"How old is she?" put in Hannah. "I am trying to picture her. Is she grey haired?"

"White. Completely white beneath her mourning cap, but I judged her to be in her early sixties. A kind gentle face, a woman who has suffered grievously. She had two sons and a daughter, Helena, who at nineteen was to have married a man chosen by the late baronet, but according to her mother, the girl was desperate to avoid a loveless marriage. Whether that precipitated what happened, who can tell?" He broke off and looked at his rapt audience.

"Do continue, doctor. We are enthralled." This was Mrs Stannard. "What happened?"

"She eloped with one of the grooms, a magician where horses were concerned, I was told. An Irishman, over here to escape the famine raging in his country. The baronet was like a maddened bull, his widow said. He had wide-ranging contacts, tracked them down and brought Helena home. She swore they had been married by a priest and their intention had been to travel to London. To give him his due the Irishman followed and the dogs were set on him, tearing him to pieces. When Helena's condition became obvious, her father planned to place her in a lunatic asylum."

Hannah was speechless with horror and it was the matron who voiced thoughts that were churning in both their minds. "Does Agnes Blair fit into this story?"

"She does. At the time she was employed by the family as housekeeper and the baronet suspected she enabled his daughter to escape. He could prove nothing but Mrs Blair was dismissed without a reference. One might say she is another victim. How long has she been here?"

"Certainly not ten years, two or three at the most. I wonder what her story has been and poor Helena's in the two years before she was admitted a decade ago," John Gidley pondered. "However, we are no nearer knowing why the child is at risk. Have you any theories, doctor?"

There was a short silence during which the only sound was the crackling and hissing of the log fire.

"It seems that Helena's younger brother, Duncan, a publisher, journalist or something along those lines, has offered a huge reward for information leading to the whereabouts of his niece. His mother has a deep longing to meet the child."

"I have met Mr Stuart-Rae," said Hannah, "but if what you say is true, he would not pose a risk to Rosa. I can see why someone treated *me* badly in a desire to obtain information if they wanted the reward, but who was it visited number fourteen and seemed to have designs upon her?"

"Dear me, what a complicated business," the master began, just as there was a loud knocking on the door panel. "Well, come in." He sounded less patient than usual.

"Mr Gidley, sir, such a to-do," The speaker was a thin faced woman who often supervised some of the girls. "The little Welsh girl is missing. Her father is beside himself."

"In a place this size she's lost her way. Come along, Hannah, we'll sort this out." Mrs Stannard rose and Hannah followed. "Who saw her last?" the matron was asking of the woman who merely shook her head.

157

Half an hour later, the female quarters had been searched thoroughly and staff volunteers were combing the male wards. Elias Williams seemed shrunken and withdrawn, a man bearing too many burdens. "I shouldn't have left her, see, but I was fetching materials from a warehouse other side of the city."

"So you'd have been gone about three hours?" Hannah asked and he nodded sorrowfully. "She wouldn't have run off, would she?"

"It's not a prison," Mrs Stannard observed. "In the summer time the old folks work the vegetable gardens and they're not fenced in, and though boys and girls have separate yards those areas are not walled. People *do* go out, you know, but I cannot see why Sairin should have left the place when she knew you were returning, Mr Williams."

It was red-headed Fran Noone who offered the first clue when she met with Hannah. "She was talking to Miss Phipps. I saw 'em, miss, in the big classroom they were and Sairin looked upset. Just before tea, miss."

"Well, where is the Phipps woman?" the matron said heatedly. "Find her, will you, someone."

Hannah was one of several staff accompanied by some of the more reliable inmates who set out to look for her without success, and finding Agnes Blair huddled in her room she spoke to her gently.

"Have you seen Miss Phipps?"

Agnes looked at the floor and shook her head. "I dinnae see anything. I dinnae ken anybody."

"This is very important. A girl is missing and she was seen with Miss Phipps late this afternoon."

"She's a snell body, sharpens her tongue every mornin' I'll be bound, but a fondness for the bonnie ones. Aye, that's Miss Martha Phipps. Out to rescue the ones that might be led astray, but I dinnae care for her, mysel."

"Did you know her before you came here? Was she employed by the Stuart-Rae family?" An unruly thought crossed Hannah's mind and she pursued it despite the urgency of her search for Sairin.

Agnes raised her head and her gaze was unblinking. "I didnae ken the besom until I came here."

That seemed straightforward enough but had the woman seen her with Sairin?

"The wee lassie was greetin'; ye ken, weepin'. They were awa' oot the door and the Phipps women saying she'd find the bairn's Da. Miss Morley, ye're a guid lass yersel', ye'll not let the master put me awa' on account o' whit I did?"

"You haven't done anything and nobody will put you away, that's a promise, Agnes. You've been very helpful." With a whisk of her skirts, Hannah was out of the door and ran until she found Mrs Stannard. "I think Miss Phipps has her." Briefly she related what Agnes had said. "They may have left the buildings."

"Thass reet enough," the porter said. "Coupla hours back. The teacher and the fair-haired lass. The little'un crying and the woman saying she'd put things reet."

"Which way did they go?" Hannah's breath steamed in the cold night air and she shivered. "Did they walk into the city?"

"They didn't walk anywhere. Hailed a cab. Not many of them around here so I noticed particular like." His thin face twitched. "I can tell you where they were headin'," he added on a triumphant note. "Friar's something or other."

Why go there? What was Miss Phipps's connection with Blackfrairs Lane, if that was where she was taking Sairin? Was she part of an organisation that abducted young girls? Of course, she had to be. That was why she had taken an interest in Molly Tinsley, and God help *that* poor girl, her thoughts ran as she dashed indoors to find Mr Gidley or Dr Marcus Lisle. Neither was to be found in the study.

"Searchin' for the lost lass," she was informed by all whom she asked. The clock was ticking and whilst she delayed, every passing minute brought danger closer to poor frightened Sairin. If she had been taken to number fourteen, she, Hannah, knew precisely where to go and how to get there.

Snatching a cape from a peg behind her bedroom door and scooping coins into a drawstring purse, she left the building and after speaking hastily to the porter, was in the road leading into the city. There was no cab in sight and few people around as she scurried along, heart hammering and feet slipping on pavements that were now frosty. *Don't let me be too late*, was her silent prayer.

Closer to the city the streets were busier. It was getting late but some shops appeared to be doing a brisk trade with the New Year celebrations but days away. Sam was in the apothecary's, grinding ingredients into powder, his head bent over a pestle and mortar, but there was no time to delay and he did not see her as she hurried past. Leaving behind the gaslight glitter she turned into the road leading to her destination and only when she came to Blackfriars Lane did she slow her steps and approach with more care. Next-door-Nellie's was unlit, according to Dr Lisle, the inhabitants having fled. Hidden by the holly hedge until she had rounded it, dim light showed through the glass front door panel of number fourteen, but to lift the brass knocker and announce her presence would be foolish.

Cursing the darkness, yet thankful for what light a sliver of moon gave in a clear sky, Hannah walked past number fourteen looking for a path that might lead to the back of the house. There was access at the side but it was overgrown with weeds and rank ferns, and the smell of decay was all about her. She would have turned back but for the faint sound of voices apparently issuing from within and crept towards a window from which shone pale flickering light. Her boot caught on a sharp stone and the echoing noise caused her to hold her breath. Conversation ceased for a minute or two and a shadow darkened the window space. Crouching low, Hannah stifled a gasp when some living creature she had disturbed shot out of the tangled weeds. Her heart hammered but she remonstrated with herself, thoughts of Sairin emboldening her resolve.

"Do it for me, Polly. Keep her here." The pleading voice was high-pitched with anxiety. "She'd be safe because it's the last place they'd look."

Polly? Surely the voice was that of Martha Phipps but who was she addressing? A step or two closer and she might be able to peer into the room and discover the identity of Polly whom Sal said had killed a baby. Polly who almost certainly had connections with Next-Door-Nellie; but what possible connection had either of them with the workhouse teacher?

She moved slowly and purposefully, pushing aside the dirty ferns and trying to keep her footing only to hear what must be a slate crack beneath her foot, the sound of a pistol shot in the gloomy shadows. The flickering light was extinguished, a child's fearful cry was cut off. Retracing her steps with utmost care Hannah stood hesitantly, indecision paralysing movement and at that moment a carriage drawn by two horses turned into Blackfrairs Lane and halted outside the house. A horse whinnied and stamped on the cobbles; someone alighted from the vehicle and approached the front door which at that moment was thrown open. Light spilled out and catching a glimpse from her hiding place she saw a male figure push aside a woman who stood on the step.

"Mr Meredith, thank goodness you are here. The child has been in the most dreadful danger..." The words were cut off and the door slammed. Across the street a couple halted and stood for a few moments as if waiting for an interesting development, then continued on their way. It was not the kind of area where people interfered in the affairs of neighbours because, as Hannah knew very well, to do so might be risky. Better to see nothing, know nothing and do nothing that would stir a pot of poison.

Sairin's pale frightened face filled her mind. Making no sense of what she had just witnessed, Hannah crept closer to the front door. There had to be a connection between Martha Phipps and Mr Jasper Meredith, but he had merely pushed her aside when she had indicated help was needed. If the child was to be transported in the waiting carriage, there would be no knowing where she might be taken and no way of following. It was imperative to know.

Now, darkness was her friend. She flitted across the front of the house and stood in the porch, her ears straining for sounds. Nothing. Holding her breath, she turned the door handle and pushed gently. The door opened silently and she entered. A green glass oil lamp stood on the table, replacing the one she had shattered when last in this miserable place. Voices were now audible and fearing discovery, Hannah moved swiftly to the foot of the stairs intending to climb to the first-floor landing. Too late, a door was opening and swiftly she darted to the side of a vast cast iron hallstand and hid in the folds of the outer garments hanging on it.

"I...really do not understand, Mr Meredith. We...that is I...I thought we were keeping the girls safe. The pretty ones. You asked me to keep an open eye for the ones who would attract the gentlemen and we would be certain they escaped harm. You said Brookwood was…"

"Hold your noise, you stupid fool. Who but you would believe such a pack of lies? I am not delaying a moment longer. The girl comes with me." There was the sound of a child's loud wail which ended on a high-pitched squeal.

"No, no, you can't take her. For a start there will be an outcry. I shall raise the alarm."

"You won't because you're coming too. Not that you'd be of use to any man but I'm not leaving you here." His voice was a sneer and in a corner of her mind, Hannah was aware of the particular cruelty of his words.

Footsteps fled along the hall and someone brushed past Hannah who buried her face in stale clothing and recollected that her boots might well be on view. With the possibility of detection her heart thudded so uncomfortably, she feared it would burst.

"Dada," Sairin's anguished cry echoed through the house and Martha Phipps was heard attempting to comfort the child.

"Keep her quiet," snarled Jasper Meredith. "And Polly, control your wretched sister."

Mrs Wilson was heard replying that she'd never been able to control Martha. Why! Hadn't she turned up on the doorstep that very evening with the girl in tow?

"Because someone tried to snatch her from the girls' exercise yard. No doubt one of your henchmen, Mr Jasper Meredith. I…I hate you. You've used me and all I wanted to do was save her."

"She'd have been safer inside the workhouse," he taunted, but Hannah was scarcely aware of his words because it was as if a light shone into the corners of her mind. Of course, Polly! It was a nickname for Mary, linked somehow with the name Molly, a derivative. How blind she had been, how lacking in perspicacity. Yet, in fairness to herself there had been no obvious tie between the two women.

Martha Phipps was cold and prim and outwardly pious, her natural instincts thwarted and her sensitivity blunted, but would she be an accessory to murder? Whereas Polly…Mary Wilson? *Polly killed a little baby.* Mary who was often absent from number fourteen, whose blanket had been blood-stained, her cuffs likewise. Had she acted as midwife in the house next door? Had she and Nellie controlled the establishment that

162

accommodated single pregnant young women and after the births arranged for the unwanted babies to be farmed out…or disposed of?

Thoughts whirled in Hannah's brain and then without warning there was a piercing cry and light running footsteps before Sairin collided with the hallstand, clutching at cloaks and coats and exposing Hannah to the amazed stares of the two women and Jasper Meredith.

****

Chapter Twenty-One

"Well, well…Miss Hannah Morley! Always where she should not be. Bold, beautiful, and a blasted nuisance. Let's get going. You too, Hannah; oh, yes, I daresay we can find something for *you* to do." His eyes raked her slender figure and it took all her courage to face him.

He turned at last and striding to the door whistled to the carriage driver who appeared within seconds; and not the usual type of driver. This man was dressed as a gentleman of taste, grey striped pantaloons exposed beneath a long coat with fashionable wide collar; but over-riding all impressions was the whiff of expensive cologne. Here was her abductor, thought Hannah, and shrank back against the hallstand.

Two women and a little girl were no match against two men and Mary Wilson, the latter blocking access to the stairs and back of the house, and within minutes they were being bundled into the smart coach; the door was slammed and the two men seated in the driving seat. Hannah tried the door but it was locked or fastened outside. A whip cracked over the backs of the straining animals as with some difficulty the vehicle turned in the street. Faces appeared at windows but the occupants were unaware and minutes later they were edging into the main thoroughfare and gathering speed. Sairin shrank back against soft leather upholstery and clutched Hannah's hand.

"Where are we going?" she whispered and Hannah tightened her grip.

"I don't know but I shall take care of you."

"Brookwood." Martha Phipps snapped out the word. "That's my guess. The other man is Mr Meredith's friend and he owns the place. I don't know his real name. He's known as Sir Adam. It's where they train…at least that's what I was led to believe…" Her voice trailed off.

"You thought girls were being trained to become a better class of servant, is that it? Did you really hope to improve their lives?"

"I did. It's what I was told. There was no reason to doubt." Even at this perilous time when there appeared no hope of escape, the other woman's tone was clipped and controlled.

Hannah pulled the child against her as the coach bounced along and she was thankful it was well sprung. A gentleman's possession and doubtless it had been costly. It was also their prison.

The window blinds were fastened up and as they passed other vehicles and pedestrians, Hannah tried to attract their attention but on the one occasion she managed it, she received a wave of a hand in return. Then they had left the city suburbs and were in the countryside, the combined strength of the two horses giving the passengers a sensation of flying, so fast were they moving.

Sairin sagged against her and Hannah hoped the girl would sleep, overcome with emotions and weariness.

"I acted for the best, you have to believe me," Martha Phipps was saying.

Hannah turned on her. "I don't have to believe anything you say. Frankly, I don't know what or who to believe. You have treated me with disdain ever since we met; you are friendly with a man who is involved in some shameful business concerning young girls; you have engineered to have certain girls taken to a place called Brookwood, and I have seen for myself that you paw the girls, playing with their hair. Why should I suppose you know the truth from a lie?"

"You don't know anything. You've never suffered. It was always Polly this and Polly that. So charming, so pretty; Polly who got herself a man."

"Polly will get herself a gaol sentence. Your sister is as embittered as you, twisted too. Whatever turned the pair of you into such fiends?"

"You're always on about your doting father; such a wonderful, compassionate, understanding parent. We were terrified of our papa. At eight years old, I fainted when I feared a reprimand and a beating from him. Our mama was a cold-hearted woman and weak; she pretended all was well but she knew, and she let him take a strap to us, time and again."

"What was his profession, or was he a landowner?"

"He was the third son of landed gentry and he was forced to go into the church. He didn't believe, he didn't care about his flock, but he kept the rules. He boxed himself in with rules and regulations. Spare the rod and spoil the child, and that sort of thing. But he enjoyed chastising us. We knew he did. It gave him power over the powerless."

It seemed she had known no warmth or affection. It explained so much about her and her sister. Mary Wilson might be past redemption but Martha Phipps may have acted in what she believed to be the best interests of her pupils.

"Your father sounds very cruel. I don't think you are entirely so, Miss Phipps, but your sister *is* cruel and probably capable of killing a baby, as Sal said."

There came a gasp from the dark interior and momentary silence. "What do you mean, Polly killed someone? Polly killed...never! Oh, Lord have mercy, they're driving too fast."

The coach rocked from side to side and Sairin stirred against Hannah. The night hung like a pall, shrouding the countryside with only the merest pinpricks of light showing here and there as if through slits in black velvet. Occasionally, when the clouds parted, faint moonlight shone on frosty fields and at the roadside remnants of snow froze as the temperature fell. Hannah pulled her cape more closely around her and the child whilst Martha Phipps huddled in a corner of the well-upholstered interior.

She seemed to have shrunk; Hannah sensed it. If she had trusted Mr Meredith then she had suffered a harsh blow, the shock of disillusionment and the toppling of an idol, but it was hard to feel pity owing to the unkindness and petty cruelties she had perpetrated. But was she innocent? Had she really believed the pretty ones were being trained for domestic duties? If so, she was an innocent abroad in a world that was often devious and corrupt. Something stirred in Hannah's mind.

"Did your pupils write sentences on paper and did you pass on what they wrote to Mr Meredith?"

"Why do you want to know? He was good enough to present us with paper and pencils for our lessons and asked that he might see the results. It's not against the law, you know."

166

"I'm not saying there was anything amiss. It's just that I received an anonymous note and when I was minding your class, the writing of one of the girls seemed familiar. Do you remember what the girls wrote?"

"I can't recall. Oh, they're going too fast," Martha Phipp's voice rose an octave. "We'll be in the ditch."

Surely by now someone would have worked out where they were being taken. The porter would have mentioned that Hannah had set out for Blackfriars Lane. Even if Mrs Wilson had left number fourteen, Dr Lisle, and Mr Gidley, who knew about Brookwood, would raise the alarm and set out to find them. Mr Meredith and his driver companion must fear pursuit as they whipped the horses to make speed.

Time ceased to have meaning as the occupants reeled from side to side and then as Hannah acknowledged her fear that Brookwood may not be their destination, the coach slowed. With narrowed eyes she peered from the window and saw they were turning into an elaborate stone gateway, pillars topped with carved gryphons, the mythical beast, half lion and half eagle. Hadn't she heard that in legend they were supposed to guard treasure?

Now the coach moved slowly along a narrow drive bordered on both sides by trees and shrubs and eventually emerged into a circular forecourt in front of a house of huge proportions, two wings having been constructed on either end of what appeared to be an early Georgian residence. Lights shone from Palladian windows in the central section whilst those to be seen in one of the extensions possessed a muted orange glow. In the other most of the windows were darkened and in only a few dim lights burned.

As the carriage drew level with the house, grooms appeared to hold the reins before taking horses and carriage to the stable block, and the two men, Jasper Meredith and his companion, jumped down and opened the door. Sairin, waking, and finding herself in a strange place, gave a sob and clung to Hannah. Martha Phipps rallied and hissed at Mister Meredith.

"You have betrayed me. You told me…" He pulled her from the vehicle and shook her roughly, his anger barely contained.

"You repulsive old sow. You were glad enough to receive a small reward every so often, cash to warm your grasping hand."

"But I put it in the poor box. I didn't keep a penny."

"Then you're a bigger fool than I thought."

Hannah could bear no more. "Leave her alone and let us go. You're the one who is repulsive."

Now, she and Sairin were pulled onto the drive by the man she was beginning to think of as Mister Cologne. Did he own this place? Were they to enter the wide front door that was half hidden behind Corinthian pillars?

"Get a move on," Jasper Meredith spoke. She was prodded again in the back.

Taking Sairin's hand, she gave a gentle squeeze before bending down and whispering, "We shall be rescued, wait and see, cariad." She remembered the word of endearment Elias Williams had used.

"Hurry up, I said." A hand poked her roughly again and her temper flared. Lifting her skirt, she kicked backwards, catching his shin.

"You bloody bitch. I'll enjoy taming *you*."

They mounted several wide steps and a door surmounted by an ornamental fanlight opened to reveal a high-ceilinged reception hall possessing black and white star patterned floor tiles and gas lamps held high on ornate wall mountings. It seemed stark, almost bare, apart from long sofas against white walls and a few oil paintings depicting sombre faced men and unsmiling women. Mr Cologne disappeared.

Wide stairs swept to an upper storey and the party was propelled towards them. How Hannah longed for Eliza's cosy kitchen or Mariah Simpson's welcoming sitting room.

Martha Phipps was silent now, her eyes downcast and her figure hunched as if she nursed a pain in the region of her heart. Perhaps she did, thought Hannah. Sairin too crept along quietly as they reached a wide landing and were led towards a white panelled door which opened as if of its own volition. A girl, slim and pretty, her breasts almost exposed in the blue lace gown she wore, ushered them into a different world.

They trod on thick soft purple carpet. There were scarlet upholstered sofas and a quilted chaise longue. From a distance came light music and laughter; some raucous as if the perpetrator had taken a few too many glasses of wine, some soft and beguiling; and somewhere someone wept.

Hannah knew immediately the type of place where she found herself and recoiled, and the child sensing her withdrawal clung more closely. Miss Phipps, Martha, as Hannah now thought of her, stared around in horrified fascination until she received a thrust that sent her forward several paces.

"Summon Marnie," Jasper Meredith ordered, and the slim girl in blue turned at his bidding, appearing a few moments later with a tall, fine-featured woman who at first glance might have been the lady of a great house, or perhaps a theatrical performer. Her fair hair was swept upwards and secured by a diamante comb. Her well-cut dress was of dark blue shimmering silk and the hand she extended was well manicured and shapely. However, on closer inspection Hannah noticed that the thick paste covering her face did not quite disguise small sores around her mouth and her long lashed grey eyes held no expression. Hannah ignored the outstretched hand and bent over Sairin.

"Come along, come along." The woman's North Country accent was barely noticeable, a mere hint, but her impatience was obvious. The two women and child were an inconvenience although had she observed it, Hannah would have seen that the dull grey eyes rested on Sairin's pretty face and hair a moment too long. Doors, each painted in a different soft hue, were positioned at regular intervals along the wide corridor in which the three stood huddled, seeking comfort from the proximity of one another.

Ahead flitted a couple of young women, skirts frilled and flounced, shapely ankles encased in black silk. Giggling and chattering they disappeared into one of the rooms and from another emerged a slightly older woman immaculately dressed in green satin as if for an evening at the opera, her glossy dark hair caught in a shimmering net. Gemstones sparkled at her throat. Evading their gaze but nodding almost imperceptibly to the woman who accompanied them, she quickened her steps as she went ahead, then turned onto a landing from which stairs descended. From below came the chink of crystal and the origin of the music they had heard when first they entered this part of the house. Now the joyless mirth was louder, floating upwards from whatever activities took place below.

"I will put them in here for now but we've a full house tonight so it won't be for long." The woman called Marnie addressed Jasper Meredith as she paused before a primrose coloured door that opened into a room that swirled with colour and was dominated by an ornate bed, gold painted curlicues framing the padded yellow satin headboard. Coals glowed in a wide marble hearth. Her cold glance rested on Martha Phipps and she remarked, "So what do you propose we do with *her?* I don't deal in waste material, Jasper." Hannah received a fleeting look from Marnie: "Cleaned up, we might make something of this one." Then her gaze lingered on Sairin. "A little beauty here, though. Well done, Jasper my dear," she added softly, her voice the hiss of a snake.

The two women and girl were pushed into the opulent room and Hannah tightened her grip on the child. Marnie and Jasper Meredith withdrew and no key was heard to turn in the lock. That meant one of two things. They would not be in the room for more than a minute or two, or any attempt at escape would be futile because Brookwood was secure.

Martha Phipps gazed at her surroundings with revulsion and Hannah thought she might be on the point of vomiting. Sairin flopped onto the bed and hid her face in folds of satin. Hannah tried the door handle and it turned.

"Don't leave us," Martha pleaded. "I insist we stay together."

"Insist all you like but this may be our only chance. Besides, Molly Tinsley might still be in this hellhole, and if she is, I have to look for her. Take care of Sairin and stop whining."

The corridor outside, well lighted with soft glowing gas lamps, was empty, but for how long? Hannah closed the door behind her and stood for a moment, considering. There were alcoves, not large but they might afford brief concealment if she was in danger of discovery. There were closed doors from behind which came whispers and moans, laughter; she could barely imagine what might be taking place behind them, and there was one, painted white, from behind which came the sound of whimpering. For a moment she stood at the head of the stairs leading to downstairs apartments but she had no intention of descending.

Molly Tinsley would not be there, but where was she, assuming she had not been passed on as if she was a piece of merchandise? If so, she might be anywhere; London perhaps, or even on the continent. What Hannah knew was limited but she had heard of a trade in girls and young women who became subject to abuse and disease, most never to return to their homes again. Her late father had encouraged Hannah to read the publications of the day and some reports had been harrowing. Of women luring girls away from a parent or guardian whilst they were distracted. Such an evil person was known as a procuress, she recalled.

The whimpering could not be ignored and Hannah crept back towards the door and turned the brass handle. The door opened. In the dim light from an oil lamp which stood on a low table, she saw the form of a young girl lying curled in the foetal position upon a wide bed decked in white flounces. A canopy of soft pale material drifted across plump pillows so that the whole appeared almost to resemble a scene from a childish fairy tale.

Swiftly Hannah crossed to the bed and laid a hand against the girl's cheek. It was cold and moist, and the thought registered that the girl might have imbibed a narcotic. If so, she would react slowly or not at all to outside stimuli.

The figure turned slightly and stared at Hannah who reached for the oil lamp and held it high, its light revealing a girl no more than twelve or thirteen years old, clothed in what resembled childish night attire, a voluminous garment, lace trimmed. Virginal. Hannah could only hope the victim was the same, but judging by the disturbed bed linen, she doubted it, and despite the effects of whatever drug had been administered, the face that looked up at her was marked by emotional trauma and deep shock.

She realised at once that the girl was incapable of obeying the slightest command and that she herself was in imminent danger of discovery. A brief glimpse of her in the corridor in her worn woollen dress and cape, and the alarm would sound. Crossing to a cupboard she peeped inside and was rewarded with the sight of several dresses hanging on a rail and she made a rapid decision.

Tearing off the dress she wore and bundling it into the cupboard, she pulled the first dress that came to hand from its hanger and pulled it over her head. As her mother would have said, it fitted where it touched, but having fastened the front buttons with trembling fingers, she tied a sash around her waist, smoothed her hair and slipped from the room.

****

Chapter Twenty-Two

In the stronger light of the wide corridor, she saw that the garment was of lilac-coloured silk, well-cut although too big. There was no time to return to the yellow door and Martha Phipps and Sairin; besides, her freedom might be the determining factor in their own eventual release.

Voices, male and female, coming closer caused her to slip into an alcove and from behind an ornate vase containing a monstrous sized fern, she watched as a dimpled girl led her companion, a young man with beaked nose and somewhat the worse for drink, along the corridor and into one of the rooms. She was about to emerge when a dainty girl, no more than nine or ten years old and dressed in the costume of a country milk maid, tripped along the corridor carrying a tray on which were two long stemmed crystal glasses and a carafe of wine.

She paused before a blue door and placing the tray on the deep purple carpet knocked three times, waited a moment and then entered. Less than half a minute later she re-emerged and Hannah wasted no time. As the blue door closed, she stepped from concealment and called to the child who turned, wide eyed. Beckoning her over, she indicated that they should both hide behind the fern.

"I gorra go," the girl whispered. "Who are yer, anyway?"

"That doesn't matter. Tell me two things. Do you know a girl named Molly, and is there a way out of here?"

The girl's mouth became a mutinous line and Hannah wanted to shake her. Instead she said, "I am a friend of Molly's and have a message for her, and I need to take her home so I have to get out."

"I think there's a Molly in the other wing. On the other side of the 'ouse. I don't know a way out at night 'cos doors are locked, but the gentlemen come and go so they must open."

"Thank you." Hannah gave the child a hug. "Better not tell anyone about me in case you get into trouble. What do you do here?" She couldn't resist asking.

"This and that. I take their coats and hats, and I get drinks and things for them to eat. That's at night. In the day I clean and tidy and help in the kitchen. It's all right."

For now, thought Hannah, but only God knew what might lie ahead for this not-so-innocent child.

The girl sped off and Hannah stood in the alcove pondering her next move. If Molly was within the almost unlighted wing, she was probably not yet part of this wicked establishment, but who could tell? Hitching the mauve gown over her shoulders to prevent it slipping, she heard again the voice of Marnie who was almost certainly the madam in this place and a softer female tone. She shrank back as Marnie and the woman dressed in green silk came into view, pausing a few feet away to talk.

"We need the room. I suggest you take the child…" This was Marnie, and her companion nodded. "I suppose if the younger woman accompanied you, the girl would make less fuss. As for the scarecrow, she's no use to us. No doubt she can be disposed of," she shrugged. "Not our problem." They were making their way towards the yellow door. Hannah leaned forward to gain a better view and then hell broke loose.

"Where's she gone? Where's the other one? Call Sir Adam. No, on second thoughts. Think woman, think, what are we going to do?"

"She can't escape. We'll search and when we find her…well, I am sure you will think of a suitable punishment, Marnie. Clean her up and throw her to the lions, so to speak. They can have their fun."

"You're a clever one. What's she worth? I wonder! Shut up…" This was to Sairin whose voice rose on a wail. "And you, keep the child quiet and follow me." Presumably this was to Martha Phipps.

The pair were hustled out of the room and Hannah tried to shrivel, willing herself to invisibility as the quartet passed close by. Sairin, her buttercup yellow hair gleaming in the gaslight, gazed around her and her mouth opened in a round 'O' as she caught a glimpse of Hannah behind the outsize potted fern.

"Han…" began the child and too late Hannah placed a finger to her lips. The three women turned their heads in her direction and seemed like a frozen tableau. Martha Phipps stared in disbelief, the other two in anger and surprise.

Acting on impulse, Hannah pushed the table and sent the potted fern over spilling soil and debris onto the carpet where some sank into the thick pile. Then she ran.

Along the corridor and to the head of the curved staircase, aware of a kerfuffle behind her as the women debated what to do in the situation.

As she rounded the bend in the wide wooden staircase that was carpeted in rich dark red, she witnessed a scene, initially pleasing to the eye, that might have been taking place in one of the great houses of England: a blazing log fire, gleaming chandeliers, elegant furniture, stylishly dressed people and pre-pubescent girls circulating with trays of amber coloured wine.

On closer inspection, although Hannah was too distressed to notice at first, the women and older girls wore gowns that exposed their breasts, their skirts slit to reveal black stockings and lace garters, and several were seated on the laps of their clients, teasing with their lips and hands.

What she *did* notice was that Dr Marcus Lisle stood on the outside of a group and was apparently deep in conversation with a girl dressed frothily in pink silk and lace. Did she pause? She could not recall, so great was the shock, but her entrance caused a disturbance which alerted him to her presence. Then he was striding across the room, a warning in his eyes.

"Well, well," he was saying, "this one looks ripe for the plucking. I could fancy spending time with her. Could that be arranged?" He was looking beyond her and turning she saw Marnie, motionless on the bottom stair, her face devoid of expression until a false brightness came into play.

She stepped forward extending a well-manicured hand, blue silk swishing around her small feet which were encased in dainty satin shoes trimmed with blue bows. "How delightful, a new face. May I enquire who introduced you to Brookwood, sir?"

Hannah's heart beat uncomfortably as Marcus Lisle took the extended hand and smiled into cold grey eyes. "I believe you are acquainted with Mr Jasper Meredith…?

Marnie appeared to relax. "Of course, so you will be aware that we cater for all tastes, whatever they may be. We have some very pleasing and refined young women to entertain and amuse our gentlemen." She arched an eyebrow and appraised him. "Perhaps Sophie or Blanche…"

The doctor inclined his head towards Hannah. "I have made my choice. The moment this young woman dashed downstairs, her hair in disarray and her dress slipping from her white shoulders, I thought, 'It shall be this one.'"

"Quite so, then. I see you are a man of impulse," she said teasingly. "Follow me, please." She glanced at Hannah who was pale as tallow despite her desperation. "May I suggest this young lady attends to her toilette and I will send for wine, sir?"

"I am a man in a hurry. Business to attend to and so on." As they followed Marnie back upstairs, he sent a glance in Hannah's direction. Unsure of herself and of him, she bent her head and refused to meet his gaze and concentrated on making sure she did not trip over the too-long lilac gown.

"Here we are, the green room, but I insist you take a complimentary drink. It will be with you in a minute or two."

They were shown into an apartment that was as fresh as a spring day. Dominated by a bed that was draped in willow-green voile the room held white painted furniture and on its walls hung delicate watercolours depicting scenes from nature, trees and fields and small birds in flight.

"Take off your dress, Hannah," ordered Marcus Lisle and she stared at him in horror. "For God's sake girl, she's coming back. She may suspect something and we have to allay her suspicions. Explanations later. Come here, let me help you." His fingers unfastened the small cloth covered buttons that ran from neck to waist and he was untying the sash when there was a light tap upon the door and both Marnie and the child dressed in bucolic fashion entered, the latter holding a tray on which resided long stemmed crystal glasses whilst Marnie held aloft a decanter filled with straw coloured liquid.

"My best dry sherry," she said, placing the decanter on a low round table and indicating that the girl place the tray beside it. She smiled slowly but only her lips moved, her eyes did not leave Marcus Lisle's face as if she sought for an answer to something that was troubling her. Hannah glanced at the child who chewed her lip and gazed at a painting of a wood warbler perched upon a twig.

"Thank you, you may leave us now." He felt in his pocket and withdrew a shining coin which he pressed into the little girl's hand. As if reluctant to leave, Marnie turned slowly before retreating and pushed the child in front of her. With swift strides Marcus Lisle was at the door and turned the key in the lock. He placed a finger to his lips and returned to Hannah's side.

"We are suspects. I am sure someone will be outside that door," he whispered. "Just as I am sure the so-called sherry wine will have been tampered with." Even as he spoke, he poured some of it into the glasses then crossed to the window and opening it tipped away their contents.

"Appearances, Hannah," he whispered, and then said loudly, "Off with it then. Come here, girl." He was pulling her dress down and she stood in her chemise and pulled off her boots. Then he said quietly, "Listen to me. I am not alone. I gained entry posing as a client. Outside, having walked the last few hundred yards are about six of us, including two constables." Then loudly: "My, but you're a beauty. Come here, do as I say. No teasing now, I am in a hurry." His mouth was against her ear and he whispered, "Time for you to protest. Go on, play your part."

"No," she shouted. "Leave me alone. I'm not what you think. I was brought here against my will. I need to escape." He gave her a thumbs up sign and encouraged, she continued, "Whoever you are sir, please listen to me."

"Not likely." He was speaking in strident tones and was most convincing to any listener, she was sure. He almost convinced her. She now whispered, "There's a young girl in the white room, almost certainly been violated. Molly Tinsley may be in the other wing. What do you propose?"

"Some of the others will be creeping to the outer door of this wing. When I leave in about twenty minutes' time, they will rush in. Others may try to enter by the main door. After that, who knows? The law has no teeth but we should be able to rescue Molly and any other young girls. Jasper Meredith and his cronies will not want adverse publicity…Time to act a part, Hannah, go on, give a little shriek!"

She obeyed and in spite of the situation was almost enjoying herself. "Oh, no," she cried, "I've never…I'm not taking that off. Sir, you can't…"

"I most certainly can." He pulled her towards the bed and they sat on the edge of it looking into one another's eyes. "You are remarkable, Hannah. Did anyone ever tell you that? A woman of character and one after my own heart."

"Is that part of the act?" she whispered and in answer he lifted her hand to his lips and kissed it.

"That would be telling." His voice was soft, his lips tender and his smile warming. "So, here we are, the reformer and the discreet Miss Morley, what shall we talk about? I know, that anomaly, Miss Phipps, but before that, you'd better give a scream or something."

Hannah opened her mouth and screamed convincingly before saying, "Get off, you brute. You're no gentleman." In an effort to control his mirth, Marcus Lisle stuffed the pale green bedspread into his mouth and Hannah clapped a hand over hers to prevent giggles from escaping. "Miss Phipps," she said at last. "What about her? She says she is innocent. She believed she was rescuing girls at risk and thought Brookwood was a place where they might be trained as domestic servants. But it doesn't explain why she took Sairin to her sister's home and not into the safety of the workhouse."

"I'm not sure it is safe. Some inmates come and go, many have criminal contacts. My feeling is the attention of Jasper Meredith soothed her lack of self-worth. She has the hall marks of a woman out of touch with her own emotions, living by a set of rules because they make her feel safe."

"At some other time, I'll tell you what she said about her father. It explains a lot. Is it time for me to scream again?"

"It's time for me to leave. You lie on the bed. Take off your chemise but I suggest you keep on your drawers and stockings. I have to say you look tantalising in dark stockings and not much else."

"Very well, doctor, but mine are thick woollen ones, not a tart's smooth silk."

"Oh, Hannah, there is nobody like you. Bye for now and take care, sweetheart."

****

Chapter Twenty-Three

She did as she was told and lay waiting for…she knew not what. If plans came to fruition, surely there would soon be noise and commotion as soon Marcus Lisle left this part of Brookwood. The party would rush in and chaos would ensue as they searched the apartments. She strained her ears to hear.

The bedroom door opened softly and Marnie tiptoed towards the bed. "Well, you deserved all you got. Now, get up, put on your dress and follow me. Quickly, there's no time to spare."

Hannah obeyed, pulling the lilac gown over her head and fastening a few of the buttons, then pushing her feet into her boots. The incongruity of her attire struck her again as she was hustled along the thickly carpeted corridor towards the white door that opened into the main part of Brookwood and the wide staircase that she and her companions had climbed only an hour or so earlier.

Yes, there below was the black and white tiled floor, the oil paintings and the elegant sofas against the walls. There too was a group of men, and good heavens! The Reverend James Christie was amongst them, his expression that of a man on a mission if ever she saw one. Marnie gasped and wheeled round, her iridescent blue silk catching the light, that and her movement at the top of the stairs causing the party to look upwards. There too was Elias Williams, his thin face drawn and pale. A man whom she thought to be a police constable bounded towards the stairs and Marnie bundled her back through the white door and into the corridor.

Further along she spied Miss Phipps and Sairin being jostled by the woman in green as they emerged from the yellow room and from nowhere in particular Jasper Meredith appeared. His eyebrows met his hairline when he saw Hannah tripping over the lilac silk in boots that had seen far better days, her tangled dark hair falling about her shoulders and a confident smile on her lips.

"So, Hannah Morley, what have you got to be so self-satisfied about, I wonder?"

He did not have long to wonder because seconds later Marcus Lisle, a constable and a couple of men unknown to Hannah rushed from below and surrounded him. For a moment he blustered but conceding defeat his arrogant pride crumpled, and he appeared lost and bewildered, as if unable to believe what was happening to him.

Hannah was propelled along the corridor and towards the other stairs which led to the ornately beautiful room where the soirée had been in full swing. Not now, however, for the music had fallen silent and so had the assembly. Men were trying to make an escape and the girls, wide-eyed and practically bare breasted, appeared to be enjoying the debacle, whispering together behind their hands, their cheeks crimson owing to excitement rather than to the application of a carmine salve. In the middle of it all was Mr John Gidley, his expression one of agitation, bafflement and disbelief as he accompanied a constable and two other men.

"It's all been a terrible mistake," Marnie was saying, a voice high-pitched with nervousness as she pushed Hannah downstairs. For a moment Hannah thought Mr Gidley might well be echoing those words. The unfortunate man did not know where to look until his gaze fell upon Hannah who was descending the stairs.

"Oh, my dear Miss Morley..." He almost fell over as he rushed towards her. "What can I say? Oh dear, oh dear." From somewhere he produced the habitual handkerchief and mopped moisture from his sweating brow.

"I am perfectly all right and so are Sairin and Miss Phipps," Hannah managed to say before she was pushed towards a door that led into a yard that was enclosed on one side by high hedges and on the other by outbuildings that she fancied were stables. As if to prove it, a small carriage rounded them and she was pushed inside to find Martha Phipps and Sairin already ensconced.

Sairin immediately burst into tears and cried for her Dada. Martha Phipps, even after all that had occurred, appeared shocked at Hannah's appearance, and for herself Hannah was past caring.

"Where are we going?" the child asked on a sob.

"Back where you came from," was Marnie's angry reply as she slammed shut the carriage door.

*****

"It is past all imagining." Hannah was installed in the Websters' kitchen with a mug of tea in her hand and Eliza was listening with wide eyes and an air of disbelief. Rosa was absent, visiting a grandmother she had never before met in her life.

"Well, after Marcus Lisle left, I lay on the bed as instructed and the madam, that's Marnie, came into the room and told me I deserved all that had happened and I thought, *oh, yes, a kiss on the hand, a few compliments and a good laugh!* But, of course, I had to pretend to be distraught. Maybe I overdid it because she lost patience and told me to get dressed and to be quick about it. As I followed her along the corridor, Mr Meredith appeared and his eyebrows disappeared into his hairline when he saw me, wearing the lilac gown, remember."

"I can hardly believe that one of the guardians was connected to that place and that he actually picked out girls to be taken there. I suppose he made sure Rosa was placed with Mrs Wilson until she was old enough for his wicked schemes. Such appalling evil."

"No doubt he and Martha Phipps arranged that, but despite everything I think she truly believed she was helping the girls. Fancy that? I mean, he gave her money and one would imagine she would question it, but she insists she gave it to the poor. When *he* knew his intrigues were on the brink of discovery, he looked like a small boy caught out in some transgression. He crumpled. Earlier he had threatened to tame me and you can imagine what *that* meant! By the time he realised the constables and Marcus were at his heels, he resembled a scared rabbit and wasn't likely to tame anybody!"

"What will happen to Martha Phipps? From what you've told me, she's had a miserable life so far."

"Who knows? She won't get a reference, that *is* certain." Hannah looked troubled.

"I have some news too." Eliza's eyes shone and her gentle misshapen lips smiled. "Mr James Christie has been very kind to

Father. He said something about making sure he was always surrounded by loving care and…" she hesitated, "that he would like to pay court to me. *Me*. Imagine that!"

"I *can* imagine it. Why wouldn't he? The man who marries you will be very blessed. I told him you were pure gold but he knew that already."

"Sam has news too. It would seem that Mr Lawson has greater faith in his abilities than is obvious to an observer. A friend of his in London, a partner in a large apothecary establishment with a wealthy clientele, is offering Sam further training and the chance of advancement. I think he will go. It would be a pity if he missed such a chance. What about you, Hannah?

"I shall return to the workhouse and carry on with my duties, but I rather think I shall concentrate on nursing rather than teaching. Mr Gidley has called a meeting for this afternoon and I shall voice that opinion. Oh, Eliza, you should have witnessed his confusion at Brookwood. I was being hustled out of the bordello and into a waiting carriage and he stood there, almost a puddle of perspiration, unsure as to whether to play his part in the rescue of "the poor young ladies", as I have heard he referred to them, or whether to make a dash for the safety of the nearby shrubberies! In future, whenever I feel downhearted, I shall picture his expression of utter perplexity and the bewilderment at finding himself in such a place, and I shall feel better instantly."

"I hope you won't ever feel downhearted, Hannah. You deserve to be happy. Really happy, I mean." Eliza rose from her chair and gave Hannah an affectionate hug.

*****

Mr Gidley's office was warm to the point of suffocation, the log fire blazing merrily and the man himself beaming kindly upon the assembled company. Both he and Mrs Stannard were seated behind the wide desk, temporarily cleared of papers and ledgers, and looking rather pleased with themselves, Hannah considered.

Apart from herself, there were present Elias Williams, Dr Marcus Lisle and Reverend James Christie.

"Well, well, well, we're here to record accurately events that pertain to the workhouse," began Mr Gidley rather pompously and not at all in his usual style. "Of course, it is shocking that one of our guardians has been involved in an evil scheme of which you are all aware. Thankfully all the poor young girls under the age of thirteen have been rescued, although some may never fully recover, psychologically that is, from their ordeal." His face was scarlet and he mopped his brow before continuing. "For those of you who are not acquainted with the most recent developments, let me assure you that a lass named Molly Tinsley is unhurt and back in our midst. Leah Rae, known also as Leary or Rosa, is to reside with the Websters, friends of Miss Morley here, that is unless she decides to make her home with her grandmother, but of course..." he halted and looked at Mrs Stannard, "Am I being long-winded, my dear?"

Her normally pale complexion took on a roseate hue. "Mr Gidley is not himself today," she informed the company. "Shall we tell them, John?" He nodded and patted her slim capable hand.

"Mrs Stannard, Mary-Anne, that is, has consented to be my wife. There, now you all know." His expression was a mixture of self-conscious embarrassment and pride, and out came his handkerchief again to dab his forehead.

"That is splendid, absolutely splendid." Marcus Lisle jumped to his feet and clapped his hands together and everyone joined in. Mary-Anne Stannard rose to her feet.

"I am going to organise a little refreshment, John," she said casting a fond look in his direction. "Some sherry wine, I think. Please continue without me."

"Where was I? I seem to have forgotten. Oh dear, oh, dear."

It was Elias Williams who inadvertently rescued him. "My Sairin is safe, thanks to you Miss Morley and Dr Lisle. But there is bad news about my wife Dilys. I fear the worst and it won't be long now. I am returning to Ruthin, see. Soon I shall be back and Mr Gidley says I may make my home here with both my girls, Bethan and Sairin."

"Mr Gidley..." Hannah spoke hesitantly. "I have been anxious about Miss Phipps. What will become of her?"

The master exchanged a glance with Elias Williams before speaking. "I too have been thinking long and hard, and I have

184

asked the good Lord to shine a light on the way ahead, so to speak. I think she is unsuited to teaching children; it does not make her or her pupils happy. But Mary-Anne tells me she is an excellent seamstress and that's where Elias comes in."

"Indeed. We have put our heads together and devised a plan, isn't it? This place is expanding. I shall need someone to teach the women to sew. Miss Phipps will have a chance to be one of my assistants."

There was a burst of activity as the door opened and Mrs Stannard entered with a tray of biscuits and small cakes, followed by a woman bearing a tray on which were glasses filled with pale amber liquid.

Hannah was reminded of Marnie and the girl dressed as a milkmaid in Brookwood and expected Marcus Lisle had the same thought.

Their eyes met and she knew she had guessed correctly. He rose and took the tray from Mrs Stannard and offered an elegant glass to Hannah. When everyone else held a long-stemmed glass which they raised to toast the workhouse master and matron, he stood beside Hannah and whispered, "To us also, Hannah. I am determined to get to know you better. You are *not* going to slip through my fingers."

"I am very glad to hear it," she whispered back, "I like to know where I stand. It saves a lot of confusion."

Later, after they stood outside the master's office he said, "My mother insists that I take you to meet her. Luncheon in the country on Sunday next, Hannah? How does that appeal?"

"As long as you are there," she smiled at him and he squeezed her hand, then bent and kissed her firmly on the lips.

****